To those who look beyond the horizon...

Books by Shanna Hatfield

FICTION

CONTEMPORARY

Love at the 20-Yard Line
The Coffee Girl
The Christmas Crusade
Learnin' the Ropes
QR Code Killer

Rodeo Romance
The Christmas Cowboy
Wrestlin' Christmas
Capturing Christmas

Grass Valley Cowboys
The Cowboy's Christmas Plan
The Cowboy's Spring Romance
The Cowboy's Summer Love
The Cowboy's Autumn Fall
The Cowboy's New Heart
The Cowboy's Last Goodbye

Women of Tenacity
A Prelude
Heart of Clay
Country Boy vs. City Girl
Not His Type

HISTORICAL

Dacey: Bride of North Carolina

Hardman Holidays
The Christmas Bargain
The Christmas Token
The Christmas Calamity
The Christmas Vow

Pendleton Petticoats
Aundy
Caterina
Ilsa
Marnie
Lacy

Baker City Brides
Crumpets and Cowpies
Thimbles and Thistles

NON-FICTION

Fifty Dates with Captain Cavedweller
Farm Girl
Recipes of Love

Savvy Entertaining
Savvy Holiday Entertaining
Savvy Spring Entertaining
Savvy Summer Entertaining
Savvy Autumn Entertaining

4

Chapter One

October 1, 1890
Asheville, North Carolina

"Well, if this ain't just a dilly-dang disaster!" Dacey Jo Butler fisted her gloved hands on her hips and stared at the ticket agent across the counter.

The man nervously fingered a sheaf of papers in front of him, tapping them to straighten the edges.

"I'm sorry, miss, but your trunk was mistakenly taken off the train back in Raleigh. It will come in on tomorrow's train. You may retrieve it then." The fussy little man pushed his glasses up on his beaked nose and tapped the stack of papers again.

"I'm much obliged, mister." Dacey relaxed her stiff posture and worked up a grin. "I'll be here tomorrow. Does the train arrive about the same time as it did today?"

"Yes, it will, Miss Butler." The agent glanced at the clock. "Don't be late, though. I can't be responsible for keeping an eye on your belongings."

Dacey nodded in agreement. "I wouldn't expect you to." The stuffy condition of the station coupled with the unseasonably warm weather made her wish she could remove her hat, gloves, and jacket and find a cool spot of shade to rest.

Instead, she pulled a telegram from her reticule and smoothed the paper on the counter. She glanced over at the little man and offered him an engaging smile. "Can you point me in the direction of where I might find Braxton Douglas? Doggone if I didn't think he'd be here to meet me, but I reckon he didn't get my letter saying I'd roll into town today."

The man's eyes narrowed and he studied her from the top of her black western hat to the dust clinging to the hem of her split riding skirt. The barest hint of a smile quirked the thin line of his mouth upward. "Braxton Douglas, is it? I can say with the upmost certainty your arrival will catch him by surprise."

Dacey frowned when he chortled then cleared his throat.

Aware of her glare, he selected a sheet of blank paper and drew a simple map on the surface. Quickly spinning it around, he gave her directions. "Follow the road through town then stay on it for about three miles. Turn left when you come to a pasture full of horses and go down that road for another mile. Take a right at the big magnolia tree up the lane to the main house. If you get lost and need directions, you'll want to ask how to get to Bramble Hall."

"Bramble Hall?" Dacey asked, studying the crude map. "What's Bramble Hall?"

"Where you'll most likely find Mr. Douglas. If he isn't home, his mother or father likely will be. Bramble Hall is the name of their plantation."

"Plantation?" Dacey squeaked. Mr. Douglas never mentioned anything about a plantation. The advertisement she'd originally read seeking a mail-order bride merely stated he was a farmer in need of a wife. The two telegrams he'd sent after she wrote a letter agreeing to be his bride hinted at a well-educated man, but no mention had been made of a plantation.

"Mercy," she whispered, feeling faint for the first time in her life.

"Are you well, miss? Your face is as pale as the runny custard Mrs. Lang serves at the boarding house." The ticket agent fanned his stack of papers at her, stirring the air around her face.

Woozy, Dacey leaned against the counter.

What had she done? Had she made the right decision in brashly agreeing to marry a man she'd never met, only corresponded with twice?

Not that she had many options available.

After escaping the lecherous clutches of her detestable stepfather, she'd traveled to Massachusetts where she'd roomed with four other girls. One of her roommates, Josephine, was the daughter of her mother's closest childhood friend. When Dacey realized she had to get away from the horrid man her mother had married, she began corresponding with the girl.

Josephine helped her get a job at a factory where all the girls worked long, hard hours sewing. Dacey loathed spending all day inside at a sewing machine even if she was a good seamstress, but the factory burned a few days after she started work.

Desperate, she followed the example of many of the other factory workers and turned to the hope of marriage to save her from her dire circumstances. A few weeks later, she stepped off the train in Asheville, North Carolina, into a world vastly different from the life she'd always known in Pendleton, Oregon.

Overwhelmed by the enormity of everything that had transpired, she glanced down at her skirt. Without her trunk of meager belongings, she had no choice but to meet her intended covered in dust and soot from the long train ride.

Why would an educated man who lived on a plantation seek out a penniless bride? What could he possibly gain from such a union?

Mind whirring with possibilities, she felt sick to her stomach. What if he turned out to be like Luther Goss, her stepfather? She'd learned from that detestable excuse of a man that people weren't always what they seemed and kind words could easily ring hollow.

Disheartened, Dacey wondered, for the hundredth time, about her future husband's appearance. There hadn't been time to exchange photographs, even if she'd had one to send, which she did not.

In the grand scheme of things, what Mr. Douglas looked like was of little importance. The state of his heart and soul held far more concern for Dacey.

Nevertheless, she pictured him as a small, bookish man of middle age. Of course, he was educated, literate, and intelligent. His stature was most likely slight, his hair thinning, and he'd probably have soft hands.

Absently, she gazed over at the ticket agent. Her vision of Braxton Douglas closely matched that of the uptight little man.

Thoughts of those soft hands touching hers made a shudder wrack over her.

On the verge of giving in to her rising panic, she wished she knew why her mother had agreed to marry Luther. If it weren't for that ill-fated decision, Dacey would be at the family ranch in Eastern Oregon, racing her horse Thunder across the rolling hills of wheat stubble, and helping the hands bring in cattle from the range before the winter snows arrived.

Instead, she stood in an unfamiliar place, about to commit her future — her very life — to a complete stranger who hadn't even possessed the good manners to meet her train. Miffed, she stuffed the telegram she'd laid on the counter back into her reticule, picked up the map the agent had drawn, and grabbed her leather valise from the floor near her feet where she'd set it earlier.

Perhaps it was providential no one waited to greet her. The walk out to Mr. Douglas' home would give her time to gather her thoughts. At the least, the walk to Bramble Hall would provide an opportunity for her temper to settle.

She turned her gaze to the ticket agent again. "I thank you for your assistance, mister..."

"Jones. My name is Earl Jones." The man offered her a genuine smile.

Dacey politely tipped her head to him. "Thank you, Mr. Jones. I'll be back tomorrow for my trunk."

"We shall see," the man said cryptically then turned his attention to the papers in his hand.

With purposeful strides, Dacey left the depot and stepped outside into the early afternoon sunshine. She breathed deeply, inhaling the scents of autumn blended with smoked meat.

Hunger gnawed at her, but she hated to spend any of her precious supply of money on a meal. However, she couldn't walk several miles on an empty stomach. Moreover, it wouldn't do at all to show up on Mr. Douglas' doorstep half-starved.

As she walked down the broad sidewalk along the town's main street, she glanced upward at telephone poles with wires stretched like ropes of licorice across the sky.

Back in Pendleton, only a few homes in town had such modern conveniences. As she continued gawking at the telephone lines, she narrowly missed bumping into a man standing in front of a business watching her.

"Begging your pardon, sir," she said, and rushed on her way when he gave her an inviting look.

Unsettled by the gleam in his eye, she hastened her step and crossed the street. A display in a store window drew her interest. She studied the latest fall fashions for women and children before moving on. Clothing boutiques, a bookshop, and a toy store rounded out a surprising selection of places to shop. A grocer's sign caught her interest. She stepped inside the store, breathing in the scents of dill, cinnamon, and cured meat.

A short, plump woman assisted several customers at a long counter, so Dacey wandered through the store. Heat flamed into her cheeks when her stomach loudly growled. Furtively glancing around, she decided no one heard the telltale sign of hunger her belly so rudely emitted.

"How may I help you, miss?" The jolly faced woman smiled her way when Dacey stepped up to the counter once the other customers left.

"If you sell by the slice, I'd like two slices of cheese, two of bread, and a slice of meat."

The woman laughed and motioned Dacey over to a case near the counter. "What I think you want is a sandwich. We have some already prepared." She opened the case and Dacey felt the cool air waft around her face. "Take your pick."

"Thank you," Dacey said. She pointed to a sandwich with a thick slice of roasted beef and cheese.

The woman took the sandwich from the chilled depths of the case and carried it to the counter, where she sat it on a square of brown paper. She fished a pickle out of a crock and wrapped it in paper then gave Dacey a long glance before disappearing down an aisle and returning with a small bottle of milk.

"The sandwich is all I need," Dacey said, opening her reticule, hesitant to spend any more than absolutely necessary on her meal.

"Don't worry about it, dearie. Our sandwiches come with a pickle and I'm adding the milk because you're new in town and look like you could use a friend."

"Thank you, ma'am." Dacey handed the woman the exact change for the sandwich. "How did you know I'm new in Asheville?"

"For one thing, you're carrying a valise and the train arrived about an hour ago." The woman's light blue eyes sparkled with mirth as she smiled. "Besides, no woman I've seen in this town wears a hat or skirt like that. Unless I'm mistaken, you're from somewhere out West."

Dacey nodded her head. "I grew up on a ranch in the West, although most recently I've been in Massachusetts." She grinned at the friendly woman. "I'm Dacey Butler."

The woman smiled again in return. "Welcome to Asheville, Dacey Butler. I'm Ellie Howell. My husband owns this store, although if you need anything, you come see me."

"I will, Mrs. Howell. It's a pleasure to meet you and I thank you for the milk." Dacey attempted to pick up her food while holding her valise in one hand.

Ellie snatched up the bottle of milk and pickle as she stepped around the counter. "There's a table back here by the window. You sit down and eat your sandwich. No one will bother you."

"Thank you, ma'am." Dacey sank onto the chair Ellie indicated with a relieved sigh and tugged off her gloves.

"You call me Ellie and we'll get along just fine." The woman set the milk and pickle on the table then hurried back to the front of the store when a bell jangled on the door.

Dacey bowed her head and offered a simple prayer over her meal then tucked into the thick sandwich and crisp pickle. She drank the milk straight from the bottle, relishing the creamy coolness as it slid down her parched throat.

When she finished, she took a handkerchief from her reticule, wiped her mouth and hands, and then picked up her gloves. Reluctantly, she pulled them back over her fingers and smoothed out the leather. With quick movements, she wadded her handkerchief into her bag and picked up the paper wrappings left from her lunch along with the empty milk bottle.

Ellie waved to a departing customer as she approached the counter. "Did you enjoy your sandwich?"

"Sure did. It was the best I've eaten in a very long time," Dacey said. In truth, she and her roommates had been careful about spending money the last few weeks as their limited funds dwindled.

Although she hated to accept what she viewed as charity, even if she planned to marry the man, Mr. Douglas had sent a train ticket along with additional funds for her trip. Through careful spending, Dacey still had a few dollars left from what he sent. She wanted to save every penny in the event Braxton Douglas turned out to be someone more like her stepfather and less like the gentleman he portrayed.

"I'm glad to hear that, Dacey. Are you going to be in town awhile?" Ellie wrapped something Dacey couldn't see in a paper packet and tied it with a piece of string.

"I hope to be here for a good long while." Dacey's voice cracked as she spoke, thinking of the finality of her plans to wed Braxton Douglas. Once she became his bride, she'd most likely never see her beloved home in Pendleton again, not that she could travel back to the ranch anyway.

"I hope you'll stop by often. I have a feeling you have all sorts of wonderful stories to share and I'd love to hear them." Ellie handed Dacey the packet. "A little something for later, in case you get hungry."

"Thank you kindly." Dacey accepted the packet and carefully tucked it into the top of her valise. "I appreciate it more than you can know."

"Oh, I remember coming to this town as a new bride and not knowing a soul. Most people who live around here are friendly, although I recommend staying away from the mountain folk up in the hills. They tend to be a little standoffish."

Dacey merely nodded, uncertain what Ellie meant by mountain folk and unsure she wanted to find out. "I best be on my way."

"Where are you heading, dearie?" Ellie asked as Dacey picked up her valise once again and moved toward the door.

"Bramble Hall."

"Bramble Hall? The Douglas place?" Ellie gave her a curious glance as they stood at the door.

"That's right. Mr. Jones at the depot drew a map for me." Dacey held out the piece of paper the man had given her.

"That's quite a walk from here, Dacey. If you wait until my son returns from making deliveries, he would be more than happy to give you a ride."

"You've been much too kind already, Ellie. I thank you, but the walk will do me good." Dacey opened the door and smiled at the woman who'd brightened her day.

"But Dacey, what on earth are you traipsing all the way..." Ellie snapped her mouth shut as a customer walked up to the open door and waited for Dacey to step outside.

Dacey tipped her head politely to both women then hurried down the walk. She admired the many colorful displays in store windows as she made her way through town.

Once she left the last of the city behind her, she pulled out the map from Mr. Jones and studied it a moment before stuffing it inside the pocket of her skirt.

By her estimation, she was close to three miles outside of town when dust stirred on the road. She watched an open carriage approach with a stone-faced older man at the reins and a handsome young man sprawled across the seat in the back. The weight of his gaze lingered on her as he passed, but he didn't direct the driver to stop.

Discomfited by his attention and something charged in the air, she continued marching down the road. A few hundred yards ahead, she noticed a large pasture full of horses and stopped to watch them.

One of the things she'd missed the most after leaving the ranch was her horses. Her father had taught her early on how to ride. She'd become one of his best hands with a horse until his tragic death sent her world spinning out of control.

After setting down her valise and removing her gloves, Dacey took out the packet of cookies Ellie had wrapped for her. Under the shade of a tree, she ate them and watched the horses graze in the pasture. Eventually, a chestnut mare wandered close to the fence.

Dacey brushed away the cookie crumbs from her skirt and hands then slowly approached the fence. With unhurried movements, she reached through the weathered wooden rails and stroked the mare's silky neck.

"Hey, girl. Aren't you a beauty?" Dacey spoke softly, gently brushing her hand over the horse's neck. A few other horses wandered close and she gave them all a friendly pat before tugging on her gloves, picking up her valise, and turning down the road her map indicated.

Unable to resist a peek, she glanced over her shoulder. The horses she'd befriended moseyed along the fence beside her, seeking more attention.

Laughing, she set down her bag then removed her gloves and hat. Determined to enjoy her last moments of freedom, she unpinned her tightly wound hair, removed her jacket, and climbed over the fence right into trouble.

Chapter Two

Braxton Douglas forked his long, tanned fingers through his black hair and glowered at the ticket agent behind the counter at the Asheville train depot.

"What do you mean 'she' isn't here? Who is the 'she' to whom you refer?" Braxton leaned against the counter and fixed the agent with a pointed glare. Mr. Jones frequently engaged in mental games that only served to test his limited tolerance. Braxton's already thinly stretched patience nearly snapped when the odd little man offered him a cocky grin as he stepped inside the depot and muttered nonsense that "she" wasn't there. He could only assume the woman in question was the one his mother sent him to retrieve.

A long-suffering sigh worked its way up from his chest and out his mouth. "Did a woman named Miss Butler get off the train today?"

"Oh, she certainly did. Seemed quite put out no one was here to greet her, too." Mr. Jones puffed out his chest and smirked at Braxton. "She appeared to be in a hurry to reach your place, so I gave her directions. She's probably sipping tea with your mother by now."

"Probably. Why mother insisted upon me escorting Miss Butler to Bramble Hall shall remain a mystery. I've never even heard her mention the woman before today. I suppose she's one of mother's cohorts in her recent endeavors with the suffrage movement." Braxton picked up the hat he'd set on the counter and settled it back on his head.

"Oh, I don't doubt Miss Butler holds very strong opinions on any number of topics, including that one," Mr. Jones said, offering Braxton a knowing look. "I predict she and your mother will get on quite famously."

"That's all I need," Braxton groused as he walked to the door. "Another female in the house, full of ideas and strange notions."

His mother wasn't the only one with a variety of opinions. In fact, Braxton was every bit as strong-willed as his mother, and determined to do things his own way. That was one reason he remained blissfully single at twenty-seven years of age.

Despite his parents' many efforts to entangle him with any number of beautiful, eligible females, he managed to escape their plots unattached, although not entirely unscathed.

If he ever lost all his sense and surrendered to his mother's urging to take a wife, he wanted a girl of his own choosing. It would take a special woman to turn his head and melt his heart. One full of fire and spirit, not the dull-witted spoiled girls his father continually introduced him to or the money-grabbing upstarts his mother knew.

No, he wanted a woman who didn't care about his wealth or social standing, one who loved only him.

Thoughts of the girl he'd seen walking down the road on his way into town filled his mind. He pictured her peculiar clothes and the innocent look on her face as she trudged along, carrying a worn leather bag in her hand.

Although she was far enough away he couldn't see the color of her eyes, he imagined they'd match the deep teal color of her jacket and unusual skirt.

If he wasn't mistaken, the hat on her head looked like one he'd seen cowboys wearing. He puzzled over why a woman would don such a thing.

Regardless, the hat and her attire seemed to fit her, fit her personality. At least what he'd glimpsed of it as they passed by.

As he returned to the carriage and Harry guided it through the streets of town, Braxton indulged in further contemplating where the girl traveled and what brought her to town.

Although she obviously wasn't someone who would mingle in his crowd, she had a pretty, fresh face. He would have remembered her had he happened to meet her on a previous occasion.

Leaning back against the cushioned leather seat, he watched the passing countryside, admiring the glory of the warm, autumn day. The temperature was so warm, he abandoned propriety and removed his jacket, setting it on the seat along with his hat. He studied his horses in the corner pasture as they drove past the fence.

When Harry turned the corner to head down their road toward Bramble Hall, Braxton's jaw dropped at the sight that met him.

"Stop the carriage!" he bellowed, grabbing onto Harry's seat for balance as he lunged to his feet.

The wheels were still turning as he jumped out of the conveyance and ran over to the fence. Astounded, he watched the girl who'd captured his interest earlier riding one of his chestnut mares bareback, without a bridle.

Small hands clung to fistfuls of the horse's mane as she rode astride. Sweet laughter floated to him on the afternoon breeze as she urged the mare into a gallop across the pasture.

If he hadn't been so enthralled by her ability to handle the horse, he might have been stunned by the fact she rode better than any man he knew.

The horse made a gentle turn and headed his direction. He knew the exact moment that she became aware of him. Her relaxed, carefree posture stiffened.

Slowly, she coaxed the mare to a walk as they neared the fence where he waited.

"What in blazes do you think you're doing?" Braxton swung over the fence in one smooth motion, carefully approaching the horse.

It started to shy, but the woman bent over and whispered in its ear before patting it on the neck and sliding to the ground.

"Riding a horse." She brushed at the back of her skirt and stared at him with a look of bold defiance. "I surmised that much was obvious."

In spite of himself, Braxton bit back a smile. Although the girl was of small stature, she possessed plenty of fire and sass.

"Who gave you permission to ride?" He attempted to pin her with a stormy glare.

The girl grinned and pointed a thumb over her shoulder at the mare she'd just ridden. "This ol' girl talked me into it. We'll share the blame."

Unable to contain his humor, Braxton chuckled. "She is quite skillful at getting her way," he said, rubbing a gentle hand over the horse's withers. "Polly has a hard time staying out of trouble."

"Polly, is it?" the girl asked, rubbing an affectionate hand over the mare's muzzle. "You're a real sweetheart, Polly."

Braxton experienced the most ridiculous desire to trade places with the horse. Aware it was crazy to entertain such thoughts, he couldn't help but wonder what it would be like to experience such a tender caress from the fascinating female.

Annoyed by his interest in the outlandish girl, he took a step back and pointed toward the road. "Didn't I see you walking earlier?"

"Yes, sir. I'm heading to Bramble Hall, but I couldn't pass by without making friends with Polly."

"I see," Braxton said, not seeing anything at all. He had no idea what the young woman would want at his home. He speculated if she sought a position as one of the house or kitchen maids. After seeing her ride the horse so free from care, he couldn't quite picture her dressed in a uniform, polishing his mother's silver or dusting the furniture.

For a moment, he studied the girl as she stared back at him. Her long, auburn hair hung in thick curls around her shoulders and down her back. He started to lift his fingers to see if it would feel like luxurious ribbons. To keep from reaching out, he stuffed his hands inside his pockets, appalled by the thoughts racing through his mind.

Despite the voice in his head warning him to look away, he took in her smooth, creamy skin, pink lips, and eyes that did, indeed, match the deep teal color of her unfamiliar attire.

Unabashedly, he watched as she buttoned a placket across the front of her skirt that hid the wide-legged trousers. No wonder she rode astride with such ease. He'd never seen the like and assumed it had to be some sort of western garb.

Curiosity eventually overrode his normal impeccable manners. "What are you wearing?" he blurted, unable to keep his thoughts contained in his head.

The woman glanced down and brushed a hand along the fabric, removing hair left behind by Polly. "It's a split skirt. I used to have a dozen of 'em before I had to up and leave the ranch."

"The ranch?" Braxton asked, confused and oddly intrigued.

"Yep. I grew up on a ranch in Eastern Oregon. Prettiest place in the world, if you ask me, which you didn't." She grinned at him and climbed over the fence.

Shocked by her lithe movements, Braxton silently observed her as she twisted her hair into a tidy bun. She jabbed in hairpins she fished from inside her skirt pocket to hold it in place. When she finished, she tugged the broad flat top black hat on her head, slipped on her jacket, and yanked on her gloves.

Politely tipping her head to him then Harry, she picked up her valise and resumed walking down the road.

"Miss! Wait, miss!" Braxton found his tongue as he swung over the fence and jogged to catch up to her as she bustled down the road toward his home.

She turned and raised an eyebrow, waiting for him to speak.

"May I give you a ride to Bramble Hall? I'm heading that direction anyway." Braxton took her elbow in his hand and guided her back to the carriage.

"I'd appreciate that, sir. I'm sore-footed, plumb exhausted, and ain't exactly sure what to expect when I get there. Thank you."

Braxton set her valise on the front seat with Harry then held out his hand to her. She accepted it with a demure nod and started to step into the carriage then suddenly stopped.

"Oh, gracious. I'll get Polly's hair all over. I think I better just walk the rest of the way." She turned to jump down, but Braxton blocked her path.

"I assure you, miss, it wouldn't be the first or the last time there was horse hair on the seat. Come along. Please?" He held onto her hand and placed his other at her elbow, giving her a slight nudge forward.

With a resigned sigh, she stepped the rest of the way into the carriage and moved over so Braxton could enter. "If you're gonna force me to ride with you, I suppose I should at least tell you my name." The smile she cast over her shoulder left Braxton fighting the urge to kiss her lips. "I'm Dacey Butler."

"Miss Butler," Braxton said, forcing a smile, wondering what business the enigmatic young woman had with his mother. From what he'd observed, the only similarities the two females had in common were a propensity for bluntness, a love of horses, and a determined spirit.

Sure her visit was tied to something that held no interest for him, Braxton didn't press her further. Rather, he questioned her about the ranch in Oregon and where she'd learned to ride so well. He picked up the hat and jacket he'd left on the seat and tossed them over her valise by Harry.

"My daddy had me on a horse before I could walk. My mother said my first word was 'ride' and by the time I was five, I could handle any horse on our place." Dacey shook her head and laughed. "The hands used to race me all the time, but after I beat every one of them, they finally gave up."

"How large was your ranch?"

"It was only a thousand acres, but we raised a bumper crop of wheat and had the best beef cattle. Our bunkhouse cook could sure wrestle up some good chow. Rowdy, our ranch foreman, kept things going after my daddy died."

Once again shocked into silence, Braxton didn't think he'd ever met a woman who spoke so honestly and unaffected. In addition, her western twang made him grin.

Harry turned the carriage up the road that lead to Braxton's home. Miss Butler's eyes widened as she took in the trees lining the lane.

"What are those?" she asked pointing a gloved finger toward one of the giant magnolias. "The trees with the leaves that look like they've been dipped in chocolate."

Braxton smiled at her unusual description. "Magnolia trees. The leaves turn deep brown in the autumn, but they truly shine in the spring when they're filled with pink magnolia flowers. The scent is remarkable. Do you have any flowering trees in Oregon?"

The answer he awaited died on her lips as she caught sight of his imposing home.

Straightening her posture, she gawked at the plantation house his grandfather had built in the 1830s. "My stars!" she whispered. "This is Bramble Hall?"

"The main house," Braxton said, trying to envision what the place looked like to someone accustomed to the landscape Dacey had described of rolling hills of wheat, pastures of fat cattle, and sagebrush-dotted land. "The horse barn is over there, to the left. Behind the house are the cottages where the help lives. And the carriage house is over there."

Dacey appeared dazed as Harry turned the carriage around in the circular drive.

She sucked in a ragged breath as they stopped, gaping upward at the three stories of the Greek revival structure. A dozen white columns stretched from the ground up to the third story, flanking the front of the house. The curve of a grand rotunda peeked around the side of the imposing home.

"This is where the Douglas family lives?" she asked, sounding unsure and a little frightened.

Braxton grinned as he helped her out of the carriage. Quickly slipping on his jacket and placing his hat on his head, he took her valise in one hand and her elbow in the other, escorting her up the sweeping staircase to the main level of the house. "My family has lived here since 1836 when construction was completed on the house. Before that, my grandparents lived in what is now our overseer's home behind the carriage house."

Dacey stumbled on the steps as she looked at the man beside her. "Your family?"

Aware he was a man of importance, she'd noticed his expensive clothing, exquisite manners and fine speech. Young, virile, and undeniably attractive, she'd wondered who he was, why he cared if she rode the horses out by the main road.

Under the assumption he was close to her age, she'd admired his strong shoulders, a somewhat unruly thatch of wavy dark hair, and square jaw covered in rakish stubble. Regardless of her interest in him, she'd never once connected him to the Douglas family. Belatedly, she realized he'd failed to provide his name when she introduced herself.

"Who are you?" she asked, grasping the railing as her head spun and her limbs trembled. She snatched the hat off her head and used it to fan her flaming cheeks.

Braxton released her elbow and took a step back. With a grand bow, he dipped in front of her, waving his hat in a courtly gesture before settling it back on his head. "Braxton James Douglas, at your service."

"You… you're Braxton Douglas?" Dacey's face drained of all color and her legs ceased to hold her. She sank onto the step, clutching the rail in her hand to keep from tumbling down the stairs they'd just climbed. The hat slipped from her fingers, but she didn't notice.

"Yes, ma'am. I am." Braxton tossed her valise up to the top of the steps then took her hands in his, pulling her to her feet. "Welcome to my home, to Bramble Hall."

"Braxton Douglas," Dacey muttered, assaulted with dizziness, fear, and surprise.

The strong, charming man before her was nothing like the bookish little fellow she'd envisioned marrying.

All too aware of her attraction to this handsome stranger, she slipped into a state of shock, clinging to Braxton's hands as the world spun around her.

Before blackness swamped her, she turned her face toward his and whispered the reason for her arrival. "I'm here to marry you."

Chapter Three

Braxton caught Dacey as she fainted. Sweeping her into his arms, he charged up the remaining steps and raced to the front door.

"Mother!" he shouted as their butler opened the portal, eyes wide in surprise as Braxton stormed inside. "Mother!"

"Mrs. Douglas is taking tea in the blue parlor this afternoon, sir," the butler said, uncertain what he could do to assist the young master of the house.

"Please bring her to the gold parlor, George. Right away," Braxton said in a somewhat quieter tone. He strode across the entry hall and entered an expansive room with cream furnishings and gold-flocked wallpaper.

Gently, he placed Dacey on a settee and stepped back from her, sure he'd misheard her before she fainted.

No doubt, his unexpected interest in her conjured such a crazy notion.

Marriage.

How utterly preposterous.

She didn't know him, didn't know anything about him. Why on earth would she travel to his home with the intention of marrying him?

Doubts gnawed at him as he contemplated the possible reasons. Every thought came back to his meddling mother.

He hurried into the entry and watched as Harry set Dacey's valise and hat inside. The driver tipped his head to Braxton before going out the front door and closing it behind him.

"Mother!" Braxton yelled again. A moment later, the woman breezed around the corner. Her skirts swished from side to side as she rushed toward him.

"My dear boy, whatever is the matter? You know bellowing about the house is completely unacceptable." Beatrice Douglas squeezed her son's hand as she looked up into his intense gray eyes.

"There's a young woman in the parlor, Miss Butler. She fainted right after uttering some nonsense about being here to marry me. I'd like an..." Astounded when his mother spun away from him and hastened into the parlor, he followed.

"Oh, she's here!" Beatrice beamed with excitement as she leaned over to study Dacey's flushed cheeks and smooth skin. Her personal maid, Caroline, ran into the room. Beatrice turned to her and waved a hand toward the hall. "Please fetch a cool cloth for her, Caroline, and a glass of water. It might be a good idea to bring the smelling salts."

When the maid disappeared, Beatrice turned back to Dacey, pleased by her arrival although not her distressed state. "She's even prettier than I imagined."

"Of what are you speaking, Mother? What have you done?" Braxton took his mother's arm in his hand, tugging her to the far side of the room. "I demand an explanation."

Indulgently, she patted his cheek and smiled. "Brax, I realize this might seem a bit... um... unconventional, but I ordered you a bride. Isn't she wonderful?"

"A what?" Braxton's voice increased in volume while his brow furrowed in anger. His mother clapped a hand over his mouth and shoved him outside onto the porch.

Quietly shutting the door behind her, she crossed her arms over her ample bosom and glared at her son. "Your preferences on the matter of taking a wife are quite clear, but I want you to wed, son. I want you to fall in love with a sweet girl and give me some grandbabies before I depart this cold, harsh world."

Scornfully, he snorted. "I'm more likely to have one foot in the grave before you, Mother. Despite whatever lies you told, I won't marry her." Braxton paced across the porch. "How dare you turn to such manipulative measures? Did you give any thought to what would happen to that poor girl when I refused to wed her, to follow through on whatever you offered her? What will she do? You can't send her back to Massachusetts and, from the little I learned, it's impossible for her to return to her home in Oregon."

"She's from Oregon? I just assumed she lived in that northern town with the factory that burned," Beatrice said, taking a seat on a white wicker chair. "That would explain her rather interesting choice of attire. Regardless, we'll make her feel at home. I'm sure once you've gotten to know her, you'll change your…"

Braxton leaned over until his face was mere inches away from his mother's. "I won't change my mind. I won't marry her. In addition, I won't have a thing to do with your schemes, Mother. I'm finished with the whole mess."

"But, son, I want…"

As he straightened to his full, impressive height, fury shot in piercing spears from his eyes. "It's not about what you want this time, Mother. I won't tell you again — I'll have nothing to do with Miss Dacey Butler or your notions of marriage. Do what you like with her, but don't expect me to make good on your promises to that poor girl."

He spun on his heel and stalked along the length of the porch.

"Son? Braxton! Come back here!"

Beatrice released a sigh and rose to her feet. She took a cleansing breath then returned to the parlor to meet her future daughter-in-law. In spite of Braxton's protests, she would see him married to the young woman or her name wasn't Beatrice Louise Jefferson Douglas.

~~*~~

Dreams of a handsome man with black hair and eyes the color of the sky before an autumn rainstorm flittered through Dacey's mind. She could feel the muscles of his chest and shoulders as he held her in his arms. The deep rumble of his voice seemed oddly comforting and enticing, making her ache to know him better, draw him closer.

A sharp, acrid smell assaulted her nose and brought her fully awake. Her eyes popped open and she looked around, disoriented.

She stared up at an ornate ceiling. As her gaze drifted down, she took in gold flocked wallpaper on the walls, expensive paintings, and rich furnishings.

A cool cloth brushed across her forehead.

"Are you well, dear?" A kind voice pulled her attention to her left. Dacey looked into the smiling face of a lovely woman with stormy gray eyes, incredibly similar to the eyes of the man in her dream.

"Where... where am I?" Dacey started to rise, but the woman pushed her back against the cushions with a gentle hand.

"Just lie still a moment, Miss Butler. Your head will stop spinning shortly, and then we'll discuss the particulars over a cup of tea. Do you enjoy a good cup of tea?" The woman motioned to someone behind her.

Dacey heard the sound of footsteps receding as they left the room.

"Let's start at the top, shall we? You're Miss Dacey Butler, is that correct?"

Dacey closed her eyes and nodded her head.

"Splendid. That's splendid." The woman brushed a stray curl away from Dacey's cheek. "Oh, you're just perfect, Dacey. Do you mind if I call you Dacey?"

"No, ma'am. That's fine." Dacey opened her eyes, relieved her head had indeed cleared. Slowly, she sat up and took in the woman sitting beside her, holding a wet cloth in her hand.

Something about her seemed familiar, yet Dacey couldn't say what tickled her memory.

"And you are?" She asked, feeling lost and entirely confused.

"I'm Beatrice Douglas. Braxton is my son."

Dacey hadn't been dreaming, after all. She really had travelled to North Carolina to marry a man who had already piqued her interest.

Beatrice dropped the cloth she held into a shallow bowl on a table in front of the settee and settled back against the cushions. "I'm ever so glad you've arrived, Dacey. Did Braxton meet your train? What did you think of him?"

"He seems very kind, and interesting to talk to, ma'am, but he didn't meet my train. I stopped to admire your horses and he found me there." Dacey glanced down at her skirt and plucked off a few stray horse hairs then worried about dropping them on the expensive carpet.

Mindful of her concern, Beatrice brushed them off her hand to the floor then squeezed her fingers. "Oh, my dear girl. I'm so sorry. He was supposed to meet you at the train. You must be exhausted and thirsty after that long walk."

"I enjoyed the walk very much. It's quite lovely here, much different from my home." Dacey dared a glance at her hostess. "But Mr. Douglas didn't seem to know who I was or why I came."

Beatrice possessed the grace to blush. "I'm afraid that's my fault. You see, my wish is for Braxton to wed. He's my only living child, and the one thing I want for him is to be happy. The brainless simpletons who run in his circle won't shelter his heart and love him as he deserves. One day, I happened upon a publication with advertisements for mail-order brides. Since Braxton refuses to choose one, I decided to locate a wife for him. I received many replies to the advertisement I placed, but yours stood out. I knew the moment I read your letter you were the one meant for my son."

"But, Mrs. Douglas…"

Beatrice patted Dacey's hand. "Beatrice. You must call me Beatrice."

Reluctantly, Dacey nodded. "Beatrice, are you saying Mr. Douglas had no idea I came here to marry him?"

"That's precisely what I'm saying." Beatrice offered her a conspiratorial wink. "That's why you and I must convince him it's a brilliant plan."

Dacey rose to her feet, ready to leave. Then she recalled she had nowhere to go. Defeated, she plopped back down. Maybe one of her roommates would have room for her once they settled into a new life.

She wasn't afraid of hard work. Perhaps she could find a job in town. Maybe the nice woman at the grocer's store would hire her.

"Oh, you poor girl. I'm sorry. This all must come as quite a shock," Beatrice said, wrapping an arm around Dacey's shoulders and pulling her against her side.

Unsettled by Beatrice's kindness, tears burned the backs of Dacey's eyes and she allowed herself to rest against the motherly woman.

Struggling to maintain her composure, the arrival of a tea tray kept her from having to say anything as Beatrice shooed away the maid and poured the tea, stirring both cream and sugar into Dacey's cup.

"There's nothing quite like a cup of tea to set things right in the world. I keep telling Braxton he needs to drink more tea. I find it a marvelous way to relax." Beatrice filled a plate with small sandwiches and sweets, handing it to Dacey.

As they sipped tea and Dacey enjoyed the delicious snack, she asked Beatrice about the town of Asheville and Bramble Hall.

"Mr. Douglas said your family has lived here since the 1830s."

Beatrice nodded and dabbed her lips with a napkin. "That's right. My father arrived in Asheville as a young man full of dreams. With the help of his dedicated workers, he built this place from nothing and married my mother. The land where this house stands was once a bramble thicket, that's how it got the name Bramble Hall. My parents started out in a wonderful two-story house where our overseer now resides. As Father accumulated more wealth and purchased additional acres, he built this house. It took three years to complete."

Dacey looked around, admiring the beauty of her surroundings, and what she could see outside the parlor window. "So you married a man named Mr. Douglas?" she asked.

"Yes, I did. I was an only child, pampered and spoiled by my parents. Young and foolish, I allowed a handsome face and charming manners to turn my head. Before I came to my senses, I'd married Daniel Douglas. His family was from old Southern money, but they lost most of their holdings during the war." Beatrice sighed before continuing. "Daniel is a good man and I do love him, but Brax and I maintain control of all business dealings. Despite his many positive attributes, my husband does not possess a head for business matters. He spends his days hunting, riding, and pretending he's a country squire while Braxton and I work with the overseer to keep this place going."

Dacey smiled with understanding. "What do you raise here at Bramble Hall?"

"Other than a devilishly handsome son?" Beatrice teased, delighted by the bright spots of pink blossoming in Dacey's cheeks.

Dacey nodded and Beatrice laughed.

"My father raised tobacco, but during the war years we had to diversify. We also grow wheat and sweet potatoes."

"I love seeing fields of wheat, golden and ripe, blowing in the breeze," Dacey said, swamped by a wave of homesickness for the ranch in Oregon.

Beatrice smiled knowingly. "It is a lovely sight, for certain. Braxton talked me into planting an apple orchard five years ago, and that's been doing well, too. We also have the horses. They are Brax's special project, although I enjoy watching him work with them."

"They're beautiful animals," Dacey said, setting down her teacup and looking at Mrs. Douglas. "The one I rode was very clever and well-trained."

"You rode one of the horses already?" Beatrice's eyebrows nearly met her hairline. There was no doubt Braxton Douglas got his dark hair and stormy eyes as well as much of his charm from his mother.

"Yes, ma'am. I didn't plan to, it just sort of happened."

Beatrice bounced slightly on the seat, like a happy schoolgirl. "Tell me all about it."

"I noticed the horses from the main road and stopped to pet several of them. They followed me when I turned the corner and started down the road that would lead me here." Dacey giggled. "The next thing I knew, I was riding across the pasture on the back of a beautiful chestnut mare."

"Polly," Beatrice said, grinning at Dacey. "She's a sweetheart."

"And so intelligent. She responded to my commands better than many horses I've ridden."

"Where did you find a bridle or saddle?" Beatrice asked, slightly perplexed.

Dacey ducked her head. "I rode her bareback." At Beatrice's astonished look, she hurried to explain. "I've done that hundreds of time at home on our ranch. That's why I mostly wear these skirts. It makes it easy to ride, if I take a notion to jump on the back of a horse."

Beatrice rose and motioned for Dacey to join her. "You may ride anytime you wish, and despite what others might say, ride however you like. Now, tell me more about your skirt."

Dacey showed the older woman how the skirt's front placket unbuttoned to allow her to straddle a horse. As they walked into the entry hall, Beatrice noticed Dacey's bag and hat on the floor.

"Where is your trunk, dear? Did Harry forget to carry it inside?"

"No, ma'am. It seems my trunk jumped off the train back in Raleigh. Mr. Jones at the depot said he'd make sure it arrived tomorrow."

"I see," Beatrice said, while her mind plotted ways to dress Dacey like a living doll. She assumed most of the girl's clothes would be far too plain and simple for her social circles. A visit to the dressmaker would be essential, particularly with the annual Harvest Ball taking place at Bramble Hall in a few weeks.

Determined to aid Dacey in adjusting to her new surroundings, Beatrice would do everything in her power to help the young woman not only fit in, but turn Braxton's stubborn head.

Beatrice picked up Dacey's hat while the girl grasped the handles of her valise. "Let's get you settled into your room, darling." The older woman led the way up a curving staircase to the third floor.

Overwhelmed by the grandeur of the home, Dacey tried not to gawk. Her gaze took in the elaborate tapestries hanging on the walls and the sparkling chandeliers overhead as she followed Beatrice up the plush carpeted steps.

At the top of the stairs, they took a few steps down a hall before Beatrice opened a door to her left. She ushered Dacey into a room that was nearly as big as the house where she grew up.

A huge four-poster bed with rich cream-colored damask coverings dominated one wall. A marble fireplace, writing desk, side chairs, fainting couch, and a bookshelf rounded out the room's furnishings.

Awed, Dacey stepped inside, admiring the soothing pale green tones of the walls and draperies. She set her valise down near the door and walked over to a window. Gently, she pushed back the lace covering the glass, admiring a sight that showcased the river meandering through the property. A long, thin door opened onto a balcony that offered additional spectacular views.

Intrigued by the landscape below her that included an elaborate flower garden with a fountain and walking paths, she jumped when Beatrice settled a hand on her back.

"You're welcome to explore the grounds all you like. Just be careful if you go wandering. We do have some poisonous snakes in the area."

A shiver of dread slithered down her spine. She could deal with vermin of all types. Spiders didn't make her flinch. She'd even faced down a bear that wandered out of the mountains onto the ranch one summer, but she couldn't abide snakes.

"It's okay, darling. Most often, they stay in the wooded areas, near rocks, or along the water." Beatrice hugged her shoulders. "No need to fret."

The woman spun her around and led her back inside. They crossed to a far wall where Beatrice led her across the room and to a space that made Dacey's mouth hang open in surprise.

"We added these to most of the bedrooms in the last few years," Beatrice said, motioning to a large bathtub in the private bathroom. "You might like to take a hot bath before we dine this evening."

"Oh, yes, ma'am. I surely would." Dacey considered how good it would feel to sink into a tub of hot water and soak her weary body.

When she'd responded to the advertisement for a mail-order bride in North Carolina, she never imagined she'd find herself in a place of such luxury. In her mind, she'd agreed to marry a simple farmer, not the only child of a family with a prosperous plantation.

She refused to dwell on the fact Braxton Douglas had no interest in marrying her. Instead, she focused her attention on making the most of her time at Bramble Hall. If she had a few minutes before dinner, she'd write letters to her roommates Josephine and Chevonne, letting them know she'd safely arrived.

"Please, Dacey, make yourself at home. I want you to feel welcome here at Bramble Hall." Beatrice hugged her again then moved to the door. "I'll send someone up to help you while I find a dress suitable for you to wear this evening."

"Thank you, kindly, ma'am."

Beatrice grasped her chin in her hand and smiled. "None of that, now. Call me Beatrice."

"Yes, ma'am."

Dacey grinned when Beatrice winked at her and exited the room in rustle of silk.

With no idea what she'd gotten herself into, part of her thrilled at the plethora of possibilities awaiting her.

Chapter Four

Dacey stood on a rug in the bathroom, drying herself with a soft towel that smelled of flowers and sunshine when she heard someone in her room.

Grateful her valise held a clean change of underclothes, she hurried to slip them on. Quickly wrapping a towel around her wet hair, she cracked open the door. A maid dressed in a crisp black uniform with a starched white apron hung a gown on a hook inside the open closet door.

Entranced by the elaborate gown, Dacey forgot to be shy. She stepped into the bedroom and hurried over to inspect the dress. Cream chiffon floated in airy layers over white figured silk while vertical rows of black velvet ribbon and lace created a striking effect.

"Good golly! That's about the fanciest thing I've ever seen," she said in awe. She reached out to touch the fabric then drew back her hand at the last moment.

"You may touch it, miss. Mrs. Douglas said the gown is yours to keep." The maid adjusted the gown on the hanger then turned to stand with her eyes on her feet.

Dacey smiled at the young woman who appeared close to her age. "I'm Dacey Butler. Nice to meet you."

"It's a pleasure to meet you, miss," the maid said, dropping into a curtsey.

Impulsively, Dacey took her hand and gave it a friendly squeeze. "What's your name?"

"Cornelia, miss." The maid kept her eyes averted, but the freckles dotting her nose and the smile lingering on her mouth hinted at a happy countenance.

"Skip the miss, part, Cornelia. I have a feeling we'll be good friends and I'm about as plain and simple as they come. No need to be formal around me."

"Yes, miss."

Dacey frowned and the girl smiled sheepishly. "I mean, Dacey. I'm not supposed to be on friendly terms with our employers or their guests, or at least that's what Caroline says."

"Who's Caroline?" Dacey asked, working the water out of her hair with the towel she'd wrapped around it.

"She's Mrs. Douglas' maid." Cornelia maneuvered Dacey in front of a dressing table and picked up a comb, carefully working out the tangles in her damp hair.

"You have such wonderful hair."

Dacey grinned at her in the mirror then made a silly face. "Most often it looks like a dust devil whipped it into a snarled mess, but I did make an effort to tame it this morning."

A quiet giggle escaped Cornelia as she finished combing Dacey's long, auburn hair and shook it out to dry. "While your hair dries, perhaps you'd like to begin dressing."

Dacey looked from Cornelia to the dress hanging on the door. "Begin dressing?"

"Yes, miss. It will require a bit of time." Cornelia motioned to a corset, hip pad, stockings, garters, and pile of petticoats on the bed.

"Oh," Dacey said, picking up the corset and fingering the pale pink damask fabric. "I reckon we better get started. I'm not accustomed to wearing all this falderol."

Cornelia bit back a grin and nodded her head. "I reckon," she said, perfectly mimicking Dacey's rural drawl.

The two girls laughed and talked as Cornelia helped Dacey dress and style her hair.

When she finished, she positioned Dacey in front of a floor-length mirror in the corner of the room.

"My stars!" Dacey gaped at her reflection. Cinched so tightly she could barely breathe, the corset made her waist appear impossibly small in the gown. As she turned in front of the mirror, she marveled at the black and white striped silk fabric falling in perfect pleats from waist to floor at the back of her gown.

Cornelia had somehow managed to corral her hair in a fashionable style on top of her head with curls caressing her neck.

"You look so lovely, miss," Cornelia said, tucking a pink rose into Dacey's hair.

"Well, I've got you to thank for that, Cornelia. You must be part magic to take an old cowhand like me and somehow manage to make me look like a lady."

Cornelia blushed, pleased by the words of praise. "You're a beautiful woman, Dacey."

"I sure feel like one in this getup." Dacey stepped away from the mirror and grinned at the maid. "Instead of admiring myself, I suppose I better find my way to the dining room."

"I'll show you, miss."

Dacey followed Cornelia down the stairs and through a doorway to a hallway she hadn't noticed earlier. They turned left and then right down another hall. Cornelia stopped outside the double doors of a large room and motioned for her to enter. "Enjoy your meal," she whispered.

"I plan to. Thank you, Cornelia."

"You're welcome." Before Dacey could say another word, the girl silently glided away, leaving her alone to enter the dining room.

After taking a fortifying breath, or as much of one as she could draw with the corset cutting off her air supply, Dacey stepped into the dining room.

Pale yellow walls appeared welcoming in the evening light. Yellow velvet drapes covered the long windows while yellow silk fabric cushioned the chairs placed around the long table. Ornate chandeliers twinkled overhead.

Dacey took a moment to stare in wonder at the lights, transfixed by their sparkle. Beatrice rushed to her side and took her hand then led her over to the table.

"Darling, I want you to meet my husband, Daniel Douglas." Beatrice beamed at her as Dacey bowed her head politely to Mr. Douglas. "Daniel, this is Dacey Butler, our special guest."

As Daniel approached her, Dacey could see where Braxton got his height and broad shoulders. The two men bore a striking resemblance, even if Braxton did share his mother's dark hair and gray eyes. There was no doubt in her mind that Daniel Douglas had been an extremely handsome man in his day since he still appeared quite attractive.

"Welcome, my dear. My wife says you'll be staying on for a while. I do hope you'll be here for the holidays. The house just comes alive at Christmastime."

"Thank you, Mr. Douglas. I haven't made plans that far into the future, but I do appreciate your invitation, sir."

Daniel took her elbow and led her to a chair at the table, seating her before turning to seat Beatrice. "Please, call me Daniel. We don't stand on a lot of formal nonsense around here."

Dacey enjoyed a pleasant meal with the couple. After dinner, they adjourned to a room filled with musical instruments. While she and Daniel listened, Beatrice played a few selections on a harp.

In all her life, Dacey didn't think she'd ever heard anything as soothing or divine. Thoroughly intrigued, she sat on the edge of her seat, raptly listening. Beatrice expertly coaxed the strings to release haunting notes that sounded almost ethereal. Goosebumps broke out on Dacey's arms as she lost herself in the music.

As Beatrice finished her performance, clapping at the doorway drew Dacey's gaze to where Braxton casually lounged against the frame.

"That was lovely as always, Mother."

"Thank you, sweetheart." Beatrice rose from her seat at the harp and held her hand out to her son. After a moment of hesitation, he walked to her and took it, leading her over to a settee positioned near the fireplace where Dacey sat, unable to mask her open look of curiosity.

"You missed dinner." Beatrice surreptitiously studied the way her son's gaze lingered on their guest.

"I wasn't hungry," Braxton lied. He'd been starving, but the last thing he wanted to do was sit across the table from Dacey, staring into her lovely eyes and wondering if the creamy curve of her cheek would feel like smooth satin beneath his fingers.

Instead, he'd gone to the kitchen and begged Cook to fix him a plate of food that he ate outside on the back porch.

In the solitude there, he mulled over his options.

He could hide out the entire time his mother insisted on Dacey staying at Bramble Hall, skulking around corners and cowering in the shadows.

Alternatively, he could boldly go through his days as he normally would, be polite to the poor girl, but maintain his stance that marriage was not for him.

Honestly, he had no idea what had gotten into his mother. He supposed he was partially to blame. In the spring, he'd spent a few weeks courting a young woman from a wealthy family his father lauded as marriageable material.

Pretty and charming on the surface, Miranda was also manipulative and one of the most mean-spirited individuals he'd ever met.

Braxton quickly tired of her incessant chatter about matters of little importance and the nasty comments she uttered about everyone. When he tried to break things off, she accused him of nefarious deeds, attempting to create a scandal. In the wake of that disaster, his father had paraded an endless stream of eligible young women past him in hopes he'd meet one that struck his fancy.

The girl currently sitting next to his mother was the only one who had struck it with such force, he still reeled from the impact.

Enthralled with Dacey, he admired the way the light from the fire created a fiery glow around her head of rich auburn curls.

Frustrated by the amorous thoughts that filled his head, Braxton shifted restlessly on the seat he'd taken near his father, scrambling for an excuse to leave the room.

Before he had the opportunity, his mother jumped to her feet and grabbed his father's hand. "Oh, Daniel, it completely slipped my mind that we need to go over the guest list for the Harvest Ball. We must send out the invitations right away."

"Let's see to it, then, Bea." Daniel stood and smiled solicitously at Dacey before he turned to Braxton. "I trust you will entertain our guest the remainder of the evening, son."

Braxton glowered at his mother but nodded his head. He knew for a fact the list had been finalized last week and the invitations sent because he'd personally gone over every detail with Beatrice.

Annoyed by her continued scheming to push Dacey at him, he simply couldn't abandon the girl on her first night in their home.

He also knew he couldn't continue to ogle her as the firelight cast a spell around her, leaving him bewitched by her beauty and rustic charm.

Abruptly getting to his feet, he offered her his hand. "If I'm not mistaken, we failed to give you a proper tour of the house earlier."

Dacey smiled and took his hand, gracefully rising to her feet. "I'm to blame for that since I keeled over on your front step. I'm mighty sorry about that, Mr. Douglas."

"Please, call me Braxton." Disturbed by the charged sensations racing up his arm at the slightest contact with the girl, he released her hand and motioned for her to precede him out of the room. As she walked, he admired the fetching way the gown swayed around her hips. "If anyone should be sorry about this misfortunate misunderstanding, it's my mother for involving you in her subterfuge."

"Don't be angry with her. She's such a dear, and she means well." Dacey stopped in the hallway and placed a hand on Braxton's arm. The heat of her fingers threatened to burn through the fabric of his jacket and shirt right down to his skin.

He stared at her hand as she suddenly jerked it back. Although he wanted to take her fingers in his, mesh their palms together, he stepped away. Common sense dictated he keep as much distance from her as possible.

"She's a calculating, plotting fraud full of chicanery," he said with a flicker of amusement in his gray eyes. "Even if her heart is in the right place, Mother's methods could use some work."

Dacey grinned and followed Braxton as he strode to the end of the hall then turned right. He showed her the library and encouraged her to read from the extensive collection of books housed there.

They walked past the office he and his mother used to maintain the plantation's business affairs. Dacey admired the twin oak desks and a bank of windows that lit the room with light from the setting sun.

"It's so beautiful here, so different," Dacey said as she gazed outside. The last of the daylight faded into the horizon in streaks of gold and coral.

"Different?" Braxton asked, stepping beside her, transfixed by the way the gilded light softened the contours of her face.

"There are so many trees here, and everything is so green, even though it's early autumn. Back home, everything is brown this time of year. Out on the ranch, we don't have many trees, except some cottonwoods by the creek."

"If you were to count them, you'd find more than a hundred different species of trees in North Carolina." He pointed out the window to the distant hills.

Dacey's eyes widened and she turned from the window. "Perhaps I can count a few while I'm here." She took a few steps toward the door of the room then stopped and looked back at Braxton. "I know you had no knowledge of my arrival or the reason for it. I won't hold you to the agreement your mother made. I intend to secure a position and will leave here as quickly as possible."

"There is no need to get in a rush or entertain notions of doing something brash," Braxton said, concerned about Dacey's welfare. The girl wasn't at fault for accepting the offer his mother made. She had no way to know a meddling, busybody placed the advertisement and not a man truly interested in finding a wife.

For the length of several heartbeats, she held his gaze. Braxton had never been so fascinated by a female in his entire life.

Finally, Dacey dropped her eyes to her skirt. "My trunk should arrive tomorrow. Do you think I could get a ride into town?"

"Of course. Harry will take you anywhere you need to go." Braxton walked with her out of the room and down the hall.

"That's a relief. I wasn't hankering to wear the same outfit too many days in a row and as pretty as this dress is, it ain't the most practical thing I've ever worn. I sure couldn't wrangle a horse in it."

Braxton chuckled. "No, indeed."

Dacey turned to study him a moment.

Unable to resist, he found himself drawn to her bright eyes and sweet smile.

"Do you know if anyone in town is hiring? I met a nice woman named Ellie Howell at the grocer's store. Maybe she would hire me."

The thought of Ernie Howell, Ellie's philandering son, setting his sights on Dacey caused intense protective feelings to surge through Braxton. Like a cavedweller, he wanted to hide Dacey away and claim her for his own. He sure didn't cotton to the idea of the town rake chasing after her.

"That won't be necessary. If you are determined to seek employment, I'm sure we can find a position for you here at Bramble Hall."

Dacey stubbornly shook her head. "That's not right. You're already giving me a place to sleep and food to eat. Your mother paid for my train ticket out here. I couldn't accept more charity from you."

"It wouldn't be charity, I assure you. One of the grooms in the horse barn took a nasty tumble and broke his arm earlier this week. I could use someone good around horses until he sufficiently recovers to return to work." Braxton started up a staircase and Dacey blindly followed, thrilled at the prospect of working with the horses.

"You promise it's a real job, not just something you're doing to be kind." She gave him an imploring look, stopping before they reached the top of the staircase.

Braxton held up his hand, as though he pledged a solemn vow. "You have my word. I'll ruthlessly work you until you're ready to drop."

"It's a deal." Dacey held out her hand and Braxton took it, shocked by the jolt that once again shot up his arm at the contact.

When Dacey yanked her hand back and stared at it, he assumed she felt the same thing.

Hurrying up the remaining steps, he turned down the hall and escorted her to her bedroom door. "Tomorrow, we'll collect your things in town, but the day after that, be prepared to work."

"Yes, sir," Dacey said with a smile, eager to be outside in the fresh air with the horses. "Good night, Braxton."

"Pleasant dreams to you, Dacey."

Chapter Five

The following morning, Braxton choked on his coffee as Beatrice sailed into the breakfast room with Dacey in tow.

He didn't know where his mother had found the gown, but the deep burgundy color set off the fiery crown of Dacey's hair and made roses bloom in her cheeks. Trimmed in black cord, the dress accented her small waist and beguiling curves.

Quickly recovering his manners, he held out a chair for Dacey as Beatrice walked around the table to sit in the chair Daniel held out for her.

"What a treat to have two such lovely ladies at our table this morning." Daniel winked at Dacey then kissed his wife's cheek. "We are most fortunate, aren't we, son?"

Braxton cleared his throat, still unsure he could speak with his tongue tied in knots by the sight of Dacey. "Yes, sir," he croaked.

After his father asked a blessing on their meal, they filled their plates from the bounty on the table.

Out of the corner of his eye, Braxton watched their guest. She spooned apple butter, made from some of his apple crop, onto her biscuit and bit into it.

When she closed her eyes to savor the tangy yet sweet spread, he grinned. "I take it you like apple butter."

Her eyes popped open and she glanced at him. "Yes, sir. I mean, I don't..." Quickly wiping her mouth on a napkin, she gathered her wits. "I don't recall ever tasting apple butter, but if that's what I just spread on my biscuit, it's delicious."

Beatrice smiled indulgently at Braxton then Dacey. "Cook makes it every year from Braxton's fine apple crop. We've plenty, so put some more on your biscuit. You've hardly enough to taste."

While the Douglas family watched, Dacey added more apple butter to her biscuit and took another bite, enthralled with the flavor.

Satisfied their guest enjoyed her meal, Beatrice and Daniel carried the conversation as they ate.

Braxton noted Dacey appeared somewhat uncomfortable in her borrowed finery.

Subconsciously, she kept tugging at the lace on her left sleeve. Each time she did, Braxton bit back a smile. No doubt, the free-spirited girl probably felt as trapped as he did each time his mother insisted he dress "appropriately" for a grand ball.

He much preferred to wear his shirt sleeves rolled up, his collar unbuttoned and no hat on his head than parade around as a southern gentleman, too good to dirty his hands. In truth, Braxton spent the vast majority of his time working directly with their overseer and employees. Just for the experience, he'd done every job on the place at least once.

While his father looked down his aristocratic nose at menial labor, Beatrice and Braxton both knew it was necessary to keep the plantation successfully functioning.

Braxton listened as his mother made plans for the day. Her proposed schedule drew a frown from Dacey.

"No, ma'am, I just can't let you do that," she said, placing her fork on the edge of her plate.

"Now, Dacey, it would be my pleasure. Besides, I should do something to make up for my deception." Beatrice tipped her head toward Braxton.

Although he felt bad for Dacey and still wondered what had inspired his mother to send for a bride on his behalf, he had no intention of marrying the girl. Too many of his friends had succumbed to feminine wiles or the opportunity to fortify their empty bank accounts by marrying a wealthy girl. The majority of them appeared to be miserable.

From what Braxton had observed, most women put on a good show, being sweet, charming and docile up until they had a ring on their finger. Once that happened, they changed into demanding, cold-hearted shrews bent on making a man spend his life suffering for simply being a man.

No matter how beautiful he found Dacey, no matter how much she intrigued him, he wouldn't give in to the temptation she unwittingly presented.

"Will you join us, son?" Beatrice asked, staring at him.

"I beg your pardon, Mother. I didn't hear the question."

Beatrice grinned and reached out to pat his arm. "That's quite understandable, son, considering the stunning views this morning."

Daniel leaned back and looked outside. "Stunning? It is overcast and looks like it might rain today. I don't see anything out of the ordinary."

Braxton glared at his mother, aware the stunning view she implied referred to Dacey, not anything outside the window. Irritated, he scowled. "What was your question, Mother?"

"Dacey and I are going into Asheville. Harry will retrieve her trunk from the depot while we visit a few shops. Would you like to accompany us, Brax?"

"A number of matters require my attention this morning, Mother. In answer to your question, I will not be able to join you." The last thing he needed was to spend the day near Dacey.

Already thoroughly captivated with the girl, he'd be completely smitten if he spent that much time in her presence.

That would never do.

Not at all.

He cleared his throat again. "However, I requested Harry collect Miss Butler's trunk when the train arrives. With that matter attended to, there isn't a need for you ladies to venture into Asheville."

"Oh, but there is, sweetheart," Beatrice said, smiling at her son. "Someone needs to introduce Dacey to our lovely little town and I fully intend to handle the responsibility."

"I don't want to be a bother," Dacey said, looking at Beatrice. "You've done far too much as it is. It really isn't necessary. If I could just get my trunk, I can be on…"

"Nonsense," Beatrice interrupted, rising to her feet. "Dacey, darling, go on to your room, freshen up, and put on the hat I had Cornelia leave for you. When you're ready, we'll head into Asheville. It's been ever so long since I had a fun day of shopping. These two men have no interest in such matters, so you'll be doing me a great favor by keeping me company."

Dacey doubted Beatrice needed her company, but she couldn't argue with the woman. Even she knew it would be impolite, and maybe more importantly, completely pointless.

Braxton and Daniel stood as Dacey and Beatrice rose and exited the room.

Before he changed his mind, Braxton hurried outside and asked Harry to bring the carriage around to the door. He busied himself far enough away from the house, he wouldn't submit to the urge to spend the day with Dacey.

Yet, he couldn't help watching as the carriage pulled away from the house and rolled down the drive. He caught Dacey eying him and tipped his head to her.

She waved and settled back against the seat with an anxious look on her face.

~~*~~

"Please, Beatrice, you've done far, far too much as it is." Dacey shook her head as the woman held out a luxurious robe in a beautiful shade of peacock blue.

"Oh, just feel it for goodness sakes," Beatrice said, lifting Dacey's hand and setting it on the soft, warm fabric. Dacey could imagine cuddling into such a wonderful robe in front of a crackling fire with a good book to read. A vision of doing so in her room at Bramble Hall made her shake her head.

Regardless of Beatrice's assurances, she had no right to be there and no business entertaining any such ideas.

The dressmaker took the robe from Beatrice and added it to a pile of purchases that left Dacey feeling indebted and unsure of herself.

Under the pretense of ordering a gown for the upcoming Harvest Ball, a ball Dacey wasn't convinced she should attend, Beatrice soon added half a dozen other gowns to the order.

Before Dacey quite knew what had happened, Beatrice accumulated a pile of purchases including two corsets, stockings, nightgowns, chemises, bloomers, and petticoats. There were gloves, a shawl, and a parasol. That last item was entirely frivolous, considering winter waited just around the corner.

"I can't accept all this." Dacey waved her hand toward the clothing on the counter.

"Please, darling, indulge me. I always wanted daughters to dress up and I have one, at least as long as you stay with us. Please allow me to buy you a few things."

"But, Beatrice, it seems so excessive, so expensive," Dacey fretted, as the woman settled a hat bedecked with velvet roses and ostrich plumes on her head.

After a slight adjustment, Beatrice stepped back with a smile. "That looks perfect. We must get that for you."

Dacey removed the hat. The dressmaker took it from her and added it to their purchases. "It ain't that I don't appreciate everything, but I..."

Beatrice shushed her. "Not another word about it, Dacey. Truly, this is the most fun I've had in a long while, so allow me to enjoy it. Please?"

For a long moment, Dacey remained silent. Finally, she released a resigned sigh. "Okay, but surely this is enough."

Beatrice laughed and looped her hand around Dacey's arm. "For now. I do believe I worked up an appetite with all that shopping. While Mrs. Vander wraps our purchases, I believe we should partake of some sustenance. There's a delightful little restaurant just down the street. After we eat, we shall see about getting you some shoes."

Three hours later, Dacey watched as Harry loaded the last of their purchases next to her trunk and they started the drive home.

She had no idea how she'd ever earn enough money to repay the Douglas family for their generosity or kindness. From her estimation, she'd have to work in their stables until she was old and gray and the debt would probably still loom over her head.

Unsettled by what she viewed as charity, she decided to write to Josephine. Her friend might offer insight into the matter. Now that she no longer had the prospect of marriage to save her from her troubles, she had to formulate a plan for her future.

Chapter Six

"How is she doing, Tom?" Braxton asked his head groom as they watched Dacey ride a gelding around a pen. The horse was one Braxton hoped to break and sell quickly.

A few weeks ago, he'd picked up three horses for practically nothing. Two of them were good, solid mounts. The third horse, however, had proved to be a dangerous mixture of jittery, stubborn, and crazy. The animal had thrown every man that climbed on his back and seemed inclined to be foul-tempered. A horse like that had no place in the herd he was building.

Tom studied Braxton for a moment before responding to his question. "Better than most. She's a natural with the horses if I ever saw one." He offered his employer a teasing grin. "I don't know where you found her, but if I were you, I wouldn't let a girl like that get away."

"Yes. Well, um... thank you for sharing your thoughts on the matter." Braxton struggled to keep his wits about him as sunshine spread golden rays across Dacey's autumn-toned tresses. The loose braid she'd created to confine her curls bounced on her back with every step the horse took.

His gaze dropped to her brown leather boots and traveled up her dark blue riding skirt. The ruffled pink blouse she wore with a short navy jacket made her appear entirely feminine despite the fact she rode the horse astride.

Even if she hadn't been so utterly enchanting in her appearance, Braxton thoroughly enjoyed observing her skill with the horses.

In the three weeks she'd stayed at Bramble Hall, Dacey had blended so seamlessly into their lives, it seemed as if she'd always been there.

Braxton had come to anticipate seeing her bright smile each morning and listened for the sound of her laughter. Often, he found himself looking for her as he worked, hoping to catch a glimpse of her riding.

Loath to admit it, he even enjoyed hearing her twang when she excitedly discussed something that stirred her interest. For the most part, Dacey had subdued most of her western slang words. He hadn't heard her say "ain't" or "dang" for more than a week.

Despite his mother's insistence that Dacey was a guest, the girl refused to sit around the house. She'd given herself a list of chores to see to every day and completed them with an enthusiasm that often made the staff smile.

Regardless of her efforts to work at Bramble Hall and pay her way, Beatrice won the argument that Dacey needed to learn additional skills in preparation of the upcoming Harvest Ball.

Beatrice engaged the services of a tutor to enhance the girl's knowledge of proper comportment and the fine art of dancing. Afternoons, the tutor helped polish her already fine manners and taught her intricate dance steps.

Evenings found Braxton admiring their guest. She was smart, witty, and often entertained them with her stories of life on a western ranch. The delicate beauty of her appearance seemed at complete odds to her tomboyish demeanor during the day.

Each morning right after breakfast, Dacey hurried out to the barn in one of her split skirts, spending hours with the horses. Although a few of his men voiced their opposition to her presence, she thrived on the work. The fact that she possessed greater skill than many of them in how to ride and train the equines created the resistance to her assistance.

Braxton rested his boot-clad foot on one of the fence poles as Dacey loped the horse around the pen and caught sight of him. A friendly wave acknowledged his presence, but she didn't stop to chat.

In fact, if Braxton didn't know better, he'd think she was avoiding him. Other than a few polite words of conversation during the meals they shared, she'd acted as if she didn't know he existed.

He shouldn't care.

In fact, he should be grateful she hadn't attempted to force him into the marriage his mother had wrongly offered on his behalf.

Rather than push the commitment, she allowed the matter to drop without any fuss. He was sure she was the only female who would have been so gracious about the entire frustrating matter.

From what he'd observed, Dacey was friendly and kind. She'd charmed nearly every male at Bramble Hall, from the boys who mucked out the stables to their stalwart butler.

Admittedly, Braxton wasn't indifferent to her either.

He looked forward to listening to the conversations she engaged in with his mother and father, even if he refused to participate.

The opportunity to watch her ride, hear the pleasing chimes of her laughter, or catch a whiff of her fragrance disrupted his work to the point he could hardly keep track of what he should be doing. Not for the first time, he wondered how Dacey always smelled of summer flowers basking in sunshine.

Determined to shove the woman from his mind and return his focus to running the plantation, Braxton slapped the gloves he held in his hand against his open palm. The loud pop the action created startled the fractious horse.

It leaped into the air and landed bucking. Dacey did a good job of handling the animal until it rapidly twisted to the side. Everyone watched as she began to lose her seat. When the horse lunged forward then unexpectedly spun to the left, she flew out of the saddle and landed in a heap a few feet away.

Braxton cleared the fence before she hit the ground, running to her. He dropped to his knees and lifted her head, brushing the silky strands of hair away from her face as she fought to take a breath. The fall had knocked the wind out of her.

Once she sucked in a gulp of air, she glowered at him.

"Sakes alive! Are you trying to bury me six feet under, you dunce? What'd you slap your dang gloves for?" Dacey pushed away his hands and sat up, rolling her neck and shoulders to make sure everything still worked. "You had to know that cantankerous cayuse would pitch a fit and put the licks in until it played out." Dacey ignored Braxton's outstretched hand and startled look at her outburst. She rose to her feet and bent one leg then the other to make sure nothing was broken.

Concluding her limbs remained unbroken and in one piece, she rounded on him again. Angrily, she shook a gloved finger beneath his nose. "I didn't peg you for a greenhorn, but you sure enough acted like one around this worthless puddin' foot." Dacey's western lingo thickened as she jabbed her thumb in the direction of the horse two of the grooms had caught. "Ain't ya got nothin' better to do than gawkin' like a pie-eyed snapperhead? Push out of my way, 'cause I ain't even close to done tanglin' with this loco sidewinder."

Braxton had no idea what Dacey had just said, but the sparks shooting from her teal-green eyes and the pink suffusing her cheeks made him want to kiss her in the worst way. His employees stood around in various stages of slack-jawed surprise that the young woman had just taken him to task for a foolish mistake, using language none of them quite understood.

No one dared confront him in such a manner, yet she'd boldly spoke her mind before she spun around and approached the horse that had dumped her in the dirt.

With a firm hand, she took the reins and swung onto the animal's back then rode him around the pen as all the men watched.

Chastised by the fact he had been at fault, Braxton climbed over the fence and disappeared inside the barn.

He needed time alone. Time to think about the havoc the brave, bright girl had wreaked in his orderly life. He'd never been as attracted to a female as he was to Dacey and her feisty spirit.

Quickly saddling a mount, he rode off for the nearby hills.

Hours in solitude helped clear his head and he returned to the house in a better frame of mind.

Eager to see Dacey, anxiety simmered in his gut when she didn't appear for dinner that evening. Cornelia delivered a message to Beatrice that she wasn't feeling well and would see them the following day.

When she didn't show up for breakfast, worry etched lines across Braxton's forehead.

Concerned, he picked at his food then excused himself halfway through the meal. He took the stairs three at a time up to the third floor and tapped on Dacey's door.

Cornelia immediately opened it.

"Is Miss Butler unwell?" Braxton asked, wanting to peer into the room to ensure she didn't suffer from some malady.

"I believe she's quite well, sir. She went down to the kitchen more than an hour ago and asked for a biscuit and apple butter before venturing outside. However, upon your inquiry she did request that I inform you or Mrs. Douglas that she has gone for a walk."

"Thank you, Cornelia." Braxton spun on his heel, hurried down the stairs and out the back door.

Ribbons of orange, gold, and pink streaked across the sky as he rushed to the stables and saddled his favorite horse.

The morning stillness surrounded him as he rode away from the buildings of the main area of the plantation toward the nearby hills.

Although the apple harvest ended weeks ago, the tart scent of the fruit still hung in the air. It mingled with the spicy, loamy aroma of earth settling down in preparation for winter.

The temperature was cool, but not cold, garnering his gratitude for the mild, sunny autumn they'd enjoyed.

Normally, they experienced several cool, rainy days, but the sun had shone nearly every day since Dacey arrived.

Mindful of his fanciful thoughts, Braxton mused that perhaps she brought the sunshine with her. If she left, he would definitely miss the light of her presence at Bramble Hall.

If he cared to admit the truth, which he most certainly did not, he couldn't imagine life without her in it.

In the short time she'd been at his home, she'd become such an integral part of it. His mother couldn't stop talking about her, and the servants adored her. Even his father seemed quite taken with her in spite of her "western" ways, as Daniel called them.

Braxton rode over the top of a rise and caught sight of Dacey sitting on a large rock, looking out over the valley below her as the sun spread welcome light across the sky.

Quietly, he dismounted and tied the reins around a branch before walking up behind the girl who had dominated his thoughts since her arrival.

"Dacey? What are you doing out here?" he asked as he sat down beside her.

Startled, she jumped and placed a hand to her chest. Once she recovered from his sudden appearance beside her, she reached over and popped him on the arm. "You practically scared me spitless, Braxton. You shouldn't sneak up on a body like that."

"I didn't sneak," he said with a grin. He removed his hat and forked his fingers through his hair out of habit before settling the hat back on his dark head. "You appeared lost in your thoughts. Are you well? You skipped dinner last night and we were worried when you didn't join us this morning."

Dacey studied him a moment. As it did every time she found herself in his presence, her mouth watered at the sight of him. Braxton was everything she'd ever dreamed of finding in a man, yet he wanted nothing to do with her.

When he ran his long, tanned fingers through his wavy, black hair, she wished she could do the same.

Covered as it was with a growth of stubble, she wanted to trace the outline of his square jaw with her kisses. Unless his mother insisted he shave, Braxton went for days without removing the dark hair on his face. Dacey didn't mind at all. She thought it gave him a rascally appearance and enhanced his already irresistible appeal.

She took in the dark gray of his topcoat, the black waistcoat, and light gray shirt he wore. The gray tones enhanced the color of his stormy eyes until the silvery orbs drew her into their depths.

Finally forcing her gaze from his, she looked over his cream riding breeches, neatly tucked into black knee-high boots.

Everything about Braxton Douglas exuded wealth and class.

Even if he'd been interested in pursuing a relationship with her, which he clearly wasn't, she was a simple ranch girl with no idea how to fit into his world.

The best she could offer him was training his horses until she figured out what to do with her life.

She couldn't go back to Oregon.

Her friends were all scrambling to start over after losing their jobs in the wake of the factory fire.

There wasn't a single person she could turn to for help.

The unbelievable generosity of the Douglas family continued to astound her, but she wouldn't allow herself to grow accustomed to it. After the holidays, she would leave, even if she had no idea where she would go.

It was because of their kindness, the way they'd opened their home and hearts to her, that she felt sick about the way she'd lost her temper at Braxton the previous day when he'd spooked the horse.

She knew he meant nothing by it, knew it was an accident, but she'd hollered at him like a bawdy girl in a saloon fight.

Mortified by her outburst, she couldn't bear the thought of facing him at dinner. She went to bed hoping things would look better in the light of a new day. When she arose that morning, she'd still been too ashamed to sit across the breakfast table from him.

Now, with the heat of his big body penetrating her side, she struggled to articulate the apology she needed to offer for her behavior.

Had she been a man, she held no doubt that Braxton would have fired her or punched her in the mouth yesterday for her disrespectful outburst. Instead, he'd walked off without a word after he made sure she wasn't injured.

Thoughts of his tender ministrations left her pensive.

"Is something wrong, Dacey?" Braxton asked, snagging her attention. He placed a gentle hand on her shoulder while questions filled his gaze.

Tears gathered in her eyes as the warmth of his touch seeped into her being.

How she wished she could rest her head against his chest and cry out all her fears and frustrations. However, that would never be acceptable or welcomed.

"Yes," she whispered, swallowing hard as she tamped down her emotions. "Something is wrong, Brax."

"What is it, Dacey Jo? What's bothering you?" Braxton started to wrap an arm around her, but she leaned away. He dropped his hand to his thigh and stared ahead as the sun speared golden shards of light through the trees.

The heavy sigh she expelled drew his focus back to her. With her face turned from him, he studied her profile — the perfection of her oval face, the richness of her auburn hair, the narrow shoulders that often strived to bear the weight of the world.

"I'm sorry about yesterday. I shouldn't have gotten mad at you and I sure as shootin' shouldn't have lost my temper. If you don't want me to work around the horses anymore, I understand. In fact, I understand if you'd like me to leave."

He watched as she brushed at a salty drop glistening on her cheek.

The urge to take her in his arms, hold her, and comfort her threatened to chase every speck of sense from his head. Rather than give in to his desires, he released a slow breath.

"You don't owe me an apology, honey. I'm the one who should apologize. My mind was elsewhere when I spooked the horse yesterday. I know he's flighty and it was pure stupidity on my part. When I saw you fly off his back..." Braxton experienced acute pain in his chest at thoughts of Dacey being seriously injured, or worse. "I'm glad you weren't hurt. Even though I had no idea what you said, I'm fairly certain I deserved every word."

Dacey grinned as she stared at him. "It was highly inappropriate for me to get so mouthy in front of your men. I'm truly sorry. I'd like to say it won't ever happen again, but sometimes my temper runs ahead of my good judgment."

Braxton chuckled. "I promise to not startle the fractious horses you're riding if you promise not to give me a verbal lambasting in front of my men. Is that a fair compromise?"

"That's a deal, buster." Dacey stuck out her hand and Braxton shook it. He wanted to hold onto it, kiss her fingers, and caress the back of it. Instead, he released it and turned his attention back to the splendid landscape in front of them. "What brought you to this particular spot?"

"It's wonderful, isn't it?" Dacey asked as she inadvertently scooted closer to him and pointed to the horizon. "I've come out here a few times, just to watch the sunrise. It's getting light so late these days, I'd miss breakfast if I did it too often."

"But you came today."

A tranquil sigh escaped her. "I just needed the peace of this place to calm my soul this morning." She grinned as she turned to him. "Do you know what I see out there?"

"I have no idea, but I bet you'll tell me."

The enthusiastic smile she gave him made his lips tingle to savor hers. She lifted a hand and waved it dramatically in front of her, pulling his attention back to the glory before them. "I see a canvas, like a painter uses. I envision God dipping his paintbrush into the beautiful shades of autumn, dabbing it over the trees and bushes. Isn't it lovely?"

"Lovely," Braxton muttered, utterly mesmerized with the girl. Unlike any other woman he knew, he couldn't think of a single person in his crowd of supposed friends who would rise early and hike miles up a hill just to watch the sun's arrival and admire God's handiwork.

About to lose his battle to keep Dacey at arm's length, he got to his feet and held a hand out to her. "Come on, Dacey. Cornelia said all you had for breakfast was a biscuit with apple butter. I'm sure I can coerce Cook into making us something if they've already put the food away from breakfast. You must be starving after skipping dinner last night then walking out here."

"I am hungry," she admitted, sliding off the rock and accepting the hand he held out to her. She'd taken only two steps when her eyes widened to the size of bread plates. With a frantic leap, she returned to the rock and danced a nervous jig that made Braxton gape at her as if she'd lost her mind.

"Snake!" she screamed, pointing to a reptile slithering beneath the edge of the rock.

In the weeks Dacey had been at Bramble Hall, he'd seen her kill mice and spiders without blinking an eye. From reports he'd received, she'd faced down raccoons, removed a bat from the carriage house, chased away a family of opossum when they tried to take up residence beneath the back porch, and disposed of a dead skunk no one else was willing to go near.

To those who'd witnessed her actions, she came across as unflappable and fearless.

Yet the sight of a snake, and a harmless one at that, sent her skittering on top of a rock, fretfully pacing across it like the reptile might somehow work its way up her riding skirt if she stood still.

Amused, he lifted a hand out to her again. "Come down from there. That snake won't hurt you. In fact, it's probably more afraid of us than you are of it." Braxton motioned for her to step off the rock.

Emphatically shaking her head, she refused. "I'm here to tell you that isn't possible. I despise snakes. Completely. And don't you dare tell me it's harmless. I don't care if it has fangs two feet long full of deadly poison or not, they are all dangerous in my opinion." She waggled her finger toward the ground near his feet. "If you think I'm setting foot down there until you kill that thing, you've got rocks rattling around in that handsome head of yours."

Braxton didn't know whether to be insulted or complimented by her words. At least she'd said he was handsome. That stroked his ego.

He bit back his humor at her uncharacteristic terror of the snake and took a step closer.

"I'm not killing the snake, so either you'll have to spend the day sitting on this rock, or…" he reached out and grabbed her around the waist, swinging her into his arms.

Instinctively, she wrapped her hands around his neck and glanced down to make sure the snake hadn't started slithering up Braxton's boots to get to her.

He laughed and held her closer against his chest. "You are something else, Miss Dacey Jo Butler."

"I am?" she asked, looking up at him. Her face, mere inches from his, made him groan inwardly. It would be so easy to sample a taste of those tempting lips, to devour her with his surging passion. Rather than surrender to his need for her, he drew a deep breath of fresh mountain air and continued walking to his horse.

If seeing a snake sent her into his arms, he might have to task some of the younger boys with gathering a few to strategically place around the yard and barn. There would be no objection from him to have an excuse to hold her as often as possible.

At the last moment, he veered off course and over to a tree covered in morning dew. Deftly, he stepped beneath a canopy of copper-toned leaves.

Dacey drew in a breath and looked around, awestruck. "What is this, Brax? What is this place?"

Reluctantly, he set her on her feet. "This is a weeping beech tree. Mother said my grandmother had it planted for her birthday when she turned sixteen. I used to come out here and pretend it was my secret spot when I was a boy. The branches create a wonderful place to hide since they cascade to the ground."

"I've never seen anything like it. It reminds me of a weeping willow, only more colorful with different leaves." Dacey reached up and stroked her fingers across the leaves.

As she studied the tree, a fanciful dream of Braxton meeting her there for an afternoon of sweet kisses filled her thoughts. Mindful of how badly she wanted him to kiss her, she needed to leave before she acted on her feelings.

She turned to go and bumped into his solid form, unaware he stood so close behind her.

His hands grasped her arms to steady her. The power of his touch caused her legs to tremble. Absently, she contemplated how she'd get back to the house when she could barely keep herself upright.

"Dacey, I…" Braxton's head lowered toward hers.

Lips aching for his kiss, she closed her eyes. His unique, manly scent filled her nose while her hands rested on the muscles of his chest.

Warmth swirled through her, from her head to her toes, as his breath brushed against her face. Foreign feelings washed over her, leaving her unsettled and uncertain.

Her eyes popped open. Resigned to doing what was right, she pushed away from him, scurrying outside into the bright morning light.

Frustrated, Braxton released a careworn sigh and followed her over to his horse. He grasped the reins in his hand and swung up to the saddle, then held out a hand to her. She took it and pulled herself up behind him, firmly wrapping her arms around his waist.

The close contact left him mentally off balance, but he relished any opportunity to have her near.

He rested his hand over hers and turned the horse toward the house. As it meandered back in the direction he'd come earlier, Braxton let his thoughts wander to what might have been.

The kiss that almost happened made him realize how much he wanted, needed to taste her lips. His grandmother's tree seemed like a perfect spot to steal a kiss, or a dozen, but Dacey pulled away at the last second.

A lack of interest hadn't held her back. The yearning shimmered in her eyes, easy for him to see.

Something else kept her emotions in check and he wouldn't rest until he discovered the reason.

Chapter Seven

Dacey caught Braxton's frown across the dinner table as Ernie Howell bragged about his exploits in coon hunting.

She'd tired of the conversation approximately a minute after it started. Ernie and his father erroneously assumed everyone held their disturbing level of interest in treeing raccoons and shooting them for sport.

Ellie Howell offered Beatrice an apologetic glance as her husband and son dominated the dinner conversation.

The first time Dacey had met Ernie, she'd pegged him for a worthless braggart who thought he had quite a way with women.

Although she didn't find him even remotely as handsome as Braxton, she'd noticed the girls in town flocked around him. They all appeared to admire Ernie's golden head and come-hither blue eyes. Somehow, they overlooked the cavalier way he treated women.

Because she liked his mother, she'd been polite to him. However, she was careful not to offer him a bit of encouragement about paying court to her.

She might be desperate to resolve her situation, but she wasn't crazy. Saddling herself to that man would mean a lifetime of heartache and irritation.

Aware that Ernie looked to her for approval as he finished his story, she smiled and courteously nodded her head.

Lest the Howell men continue their gruesome tales, Daniel quickly gained control of the conversation, asking about the grocer business. Ellie appeared relieved as her husband and son shifted from talking about hunting to the store.

In the weeks Dacey had stayed at Bramble Hall, the Douglas family often entertained guests. Even so, she thought it strange Beatrice invited the Howell family to dine with them. Aside from the high regard most everyone held for Ellie, she didn't get the idea anyone was fond of Mr. Howell or Ernie.

Regardless of the reason for the invitation, Dacey would do her best to be gracious to the guests, even if she still considered herself one.

Beatrice assured her she didn't want her ever to leave. However, Dacey couldn't imagine they'd continue to allow her to work with the horses and help with chores indefinitely.

In fact, she knew Beatrice preferred she not do any work, but she insisted on doing something to help pay her way.

Thoughts of all the money Beatrice had spent on clothing for her caused her throat to go dry. Dacey sipped water from a crystal goblet and refocused her attention on the conversation.

When Braxton caught her eye and made a comical face, she bit her lip to keep from laughing aloud. Often, he made a small gesture or offered a whispered word in passing that made her feel like part of the family, as if she belonged, even if she never would. He'd gone out of his way to ensure she felt included throughout the evening.

After dinner, they all retired to the music room where Beatrice played several selections on the piano. When she finished, servants carried in dessert and tea.

Ernie somehow finagled his way into a seat beside Dacey. As he leaned across her to pick up a piece of pie from the tray in front of her, his hand brushed against her legs and touched her knee. She frowned at his inappropriate action.

Despite growing up half-wild on her father's ranch, her mother had instilled in her good manners, even if she couldn't completely eradicate western slang from her speech.

Appalled by Ernie's bold advances, Dacey teetered on the verge of giving him a shove onto the floor. She happened to catch a wrathful look on Braxton's face. He studied them from where he leaned against the fireplace mantle.

Suddenly inspired by the thought he might care for her a little, she inched closer to Ernie.

The muscles in Braxton's jaw tightened. Angry sparks shot from his eyes, piercing Ernie, although the dunce failed to notice.

Braxton grabbed the poker and jabbed at the logs snapping and popping in the fireplace. When he turned back to face their guests, he appeared calm once again.

He even offered an affable smile to their guests. "You gentlemen might like to see something I recently acquired. Would you care to join me?"

Ernie and his father immediately rose to their feet, following Braxton and Daniel from the room.

Relieved, Dacey watched them leave then leaned back against the cushions of the settee with a soft sigh.

Beatrice moved to sit beside her and the three women visited as they ate slices of pie.

"Did I hear correctly that you grew up near Pendleton, Oregon, Dacey?" Ellie asked as she set down her empty plate and took a sip of tea.

"That's correct."

"What made you leave?" Ellie innocently asked.

Beatrice shot Ellie a guarded look, but the question hung in the air until Dacey set down her teacup and looked at her. "The man my mother married."

"Oh, I didn't realize... I'm sorry, Dacey. There's no need to say anything further." Distraught that she might have offended the girl, Ellie shot Dacey a sympathetic glance.

Dacey waved a hand at her in a placating motion and smiled. "There's nothing you need to apologize for, Ellie. My father died when his horse threw him. Broke his neck. Mother didn't trust me and our hands to keep the ranch going, so she married the first man who asked. If he could have, Daddy would have risen from the dead and pitched a royal fit. Luther Goss is about three levels lower than a snake's underbelly, but that fact was one we didn't discover until after he'd talked my mother into marrying him."

"So he charmed his way into your grieving mother's good graces?" Beatrice asked, hoping Dacey would continue her story.

"You could say that. My daddy had only been gone a month when Mother up and married ol' Luther. It caused quite a scandal in town, even if the rules of society are a little more relaxed there than here." Dacey tugged at the lace on the sleeve of her dress. As much as it irritated her, she'd considered taking the scissors to it a few times. However, the gown was expensive and Beatrice seemed to favor it, so she refrained.

"Then what happened?" Ellie asked, gazing at her with interest. "How did you discover he wasn't the man he claimed to be?"

Dacey grinned and leaned forward in her seat. "Only a few weeks after he married my mother and moved out to the ranch, he started disappearing right after supper. He typically had a drink or two with the meal, but he'd be rip-roaring drunk when he arrived home after his nocturnal adventures. The hands and I got to wondering what he was up to. We had a pretty good idea, so one evening I followed him."

"You didn't!" Beatrice gawked at Dacey, placing a hand on her arm.

"I did." Dacey squeezed Beatrice's hand. "I stayed far enough behind the drunken lout he had no idea I was trailing him, but I followed him into Pendleton just to see what sort of tomfoolery he engaged in of an evening."

"Where did he go?" Ellie questioned, enthralled with Dacey's story.

"Had he wandered into a saloon, I wouldn't have been surprised at all. The boys and I expected that. But my jaw dangled open like the hinges had come plumb loose when I rode around a corner and saw him boldly march up the stairs to the most notorious bordello in town. One thing we've got in abundance in Pendleton are saloons and houses of ill repute."

Ellie gasped and clutched a hand to her chest while Beatrice stared at her in surprise.

Genteel women weren't supposed to know bordellos existed, let alone speak of them.

Due to that fact, both women eagerly awaited the continuation of Dacey's tale. When the girl continued to pause, studying their appalled reactions, Beatrice tapped her hand. "A house of ill repute, you say?"

"The fellas at the ranch refer to Miss Clementine's place as the twenty-three steps to heaven. In my opinion, it's more like twenty-three steps to the depths of he..."

Laughter from the doorway drew the gazes of the three women across the room. Braxton leaned against the wall near the doorway, clearly amused by Dacey's story.

"Please don't stop on my account. By all means, continue," Braxton said, pushing away from the wall and crossing the room in a few long strides. He took a seat on a side chair near Dacey and offered her an encouraging nod. "Go on."

Nervous in his presence, Dacey shook her head. "I think I've said enough."

"You most certainly have not." Beatrice nudged her side with her elbow. "Finish the story. Please?"

Dacey smiled and slowly nodded her head. "Well, I slid off Thunder, that's my horse, and tied the reins to a hitching post around the corner. Quietly, I started creeping up those steps. I remember the wood was polished and shiny, and flowery perfume floated in the air. The walls leading up the stairs held numerous paintings of..." Dacey glanced over at Braxton. Her gaze fell to her lap as her cheeks pinked from embarrassment.

"Of what?" Ellie asked, eyes round and wide.

Dacey dropped her voice to just above a whisper. "Women without a stitch of clothing. My stars, but it was the most disgusting thing I've ever seen." Dacey sat back and cleared her throat, appearing to shake off the memories of the images. "I was halfway up those steps when a hand grabbed me around the waist while another clamped over my mouth. Our ranch foreman, Rowdy, dragged me down the stairs and back to my horse. When he let me go, he said, 'Dacey! What in tarnation are you doing?' and I said, 'Finding out where that stinkin' polecat is spending all our money.' Of course, he sent me home. He stayed long enough to discover Luther spent every evening at one of the, um... establishments in town. He'd been drinking, gambling, and availing himself of the services most every night. That's how he lost our ranch."

"In a card game?" Braxton asked, leaning forward with his elbows on his knees.

Dacey nodded her head as tears pricked her eyes.

From what little she had shared about her life in Oregon, Braxton had gathered her stepfather had lost the ranch her father worked so hard to wrestle from the sagebrush, but he had no idea it had been in a drunken card game at a bordello.

"Then what happened?" Ellie asked, touched by Dacey's account.

"The man who won the ranch kept on the hands, but Mother, Luther and I had to leave. He would have let me stay, but I couldn't abandon my mother. Not to Luther. Riding away from the ranch, knowing I'd never be back was one of the hardest things I ever did." Dacey sniffled and tamped down her tears. "We moved into a tiny little place in town. Mother took in mending and ironing to make a little money while I went to work for one of my father's friends training his horses. Luther refused to work or give up his proclivity for um... well... Anyway, my mother withered right before our eyes. Within a year from her wedding to Luther, she'd passed away. Before she died, I could see things would end badly with Luther. I contacted the daughter of Mother's childhood friend to see if she could help me find work far away from Pendleton. Josephine encouraged me to join her in Massachusetts where she worked in a factory. I started making plans to leave. The day we buried my mother next to my father, Luther informed me that with her gone, he expected me to take over all of her wifely duties."

Ellie and Beatrice shared horrified looks while Braxton's hands clenched into fists. If he ever encountered Luther, he might throttle the man with his bare hands.

Beatrice settled an arm around Dacey and gave her a comforting hug. "You don't need to finish the story."

"Oh, but the last part is good." Dacey patted Beatrice's hand in a comforting gesture. "When Luther came back to the house that night, I was ready. I clunked him over the head with a chunk of firewood, hogtied him to the bed, and emptied his pockets of the money that never belonged to him in the first place. My bags were already packed and I caught the morning train east. I'd only been at the factory a few days when it tragically caught fire and we all lost our jobs." Dacey grinned at Beatrice. "Then I found my way here."

"And we're so glad you did, darling." Beatrice hugged her again and kissed her cheek. "We all are so glad you did."

Ellie hopped up from her seat and gave Dacey a hug before returning to her chair.

When Dacey looked at Braxton, he offered her a tender smile and nodded his head, agreeing with his mother. No matter how she came to be at Bramble Hall, Braxton was thoroughly pleased she was there.

The sound of footsteps drew their attention to the doorway.

"I say, that is quite a remarkable piece of equipment, Braxton," Mr. Howell said. He, Ernie and Daniel returned to the room after looking through the new telescope Braxton had purchased and set on the topmost balcony to gaze at the sky.

With a full moon overhead, it provided a perfect distraction to keep Ernie away from Dacey for a while.

Braxton had quickly lost interest in hearing Ernie and Mr. Howell brag while they looked at the night sky and returned inside. He'd listened to far more of the conversation taking place among the women than they realized. If he hadn't been so amused by Dacey's story, he would have gone unnoticed longer.

He could just picture her sneaking up the steps at a bawdy house and the ranch foreman dragging her away.

Later, once the Howell family departed, Beatrice and Daniel excused themselves for the evening, leaving Braxton and Dacey alone in the front entry.

"Is he a good man, Dacey?" he asked as they strolled across the entry toward the stairs.

"Who?" Confused, she looked at him.

"The man who won your ranch in the card game? Will he take good care of it? Of your ranch hands?"

Dacey shrugged. "He isn't a bad man like Luther, but I don't think he really wanted the ranch. He has his own place on the other side of town and it would be hard for him to take care of both. Most likely, she sold it to someone else." Slowly, she meandered her way up the stairs to the third floor. "It breaks my heart to think of all the blood and sweat my father put into building up the ranch for nothing. If Mother hadn't been so worried, so weak..."

Abruptly, Dacey snapped her mouth shut.

Although she wouldn't say anything negative about her mother, Braxton could read Dacey's thoughts.

He'd thought them himself. The woman hadn't trusted Dacey to handle the job her father had spent years training her to do in his absence. Instead, she ran to the first man she could find to take over without a thought to the consequences.

With insight, Braxton stopped at the top of the stairs and grasped Dacey's chin in his hand, lifting it so she looked into his face. "It's okay to be angry and disappointed with her, honey. What your mother did wasn't fair to you, to everything your father worked to build."

Dacey shook her head and pulled away, on the verge of tears. Rather than let her go, Braxton wrapped his arms around her in a hug.

All the emotion she'd bottled up since the day her mother announced her plans to wed Luther Goss surged to the surface, seeking release.

She hadn't cried when the horrible man took over their home, when he lost the ranch, or her mother died.

Sentiment wasn't something she'd had the time or energy to express when Luther tossed out his despicable threats. Before he could make good on them, she poured all her efforts into running away.

Tears were kept in check as she traveled across the country to start a new life, only to lose her job a few days later when the factory burned.

With dry eyes, she'd accepted the proposal of a stranger and found herself in Asheville, North Carolina. Even when she'd discovered Beatrice's deception and no husband awaiting her, she hadn't cried.

Yet, she struggled to maintain her control with Braxton holding her so caringly and telling her she had every right to be upset with the stupid choices her mother made. Choices that left her homeless and at the mercy of strangers.

From deep inside her soul, the fear, frustration, anger, doubt, and heartache bubbled to the surface, spilling out in salty tears and anguished sobs.

Unable to stop, Dacey clung to Braxton as she cried out the bitterness, pain, and disappointment.

Nearly undone by her raw emotion, Braxton lifted her in his arms and carried her to a bench in the hall where he sat with her across his lap. He let her cry until she'd soaked the front of his shirt with her tears.

Upon hearing the heart-wrenching sobs, Beatrice hurried toward them, but Braxton gave her a look that let her know he would handle the situation.

Soundlessly, she retreated to her bedroom, secretly pleased by her son's affectionate care of Dacey.

Although she hated to see Dacey in such a state of distress, Beatrice smiled as she thought how well the evening had gone. Just as she planned, the bothersome presence of Ernie Howell and his blatant interest in making Dacey his next conquest had stirred every protective instinct Braxton possessed.

With a little more effort on her part, Beatrice was sure he would realize what she'd known all along — Dacey was the one meant to be his bride.

Chapter Eight

Leisurely stretching in her bed, Dacey slowly opened her eyes, feeling better than she had in a very long time.

The weight that had pressed against her very soul seemed to have dissipated as she sat up. Without the burden of it, she hopped out of bed, skipped across the floor, and pushed the button that bathed the room in soft light.

Continually amazed by the wonder of electricity, she jigged her way to the closet. As recollections of the previous evening flooded over her with sudden clarity, she tripped on the rug and caught herself on a chair.

What had she done?

Not only had she shared the whole story of her past, but she'd also soaked Braxton's shirt with her tears, sobbing like a helpless baby.

He'd held her and crooned words of comfort until she was so spent, she slumped against him in exhaustion.

With great care, he'd carried her into her bedroom and summoned Cornelia to help her undress. Once she was ensconced beneath the warm covers, he returned to the room and tenderly brushed the hair back from her face, staying with her until she fell asleep.

Mortified that she'd broken down in front of Braxton, of all people, and let him tuck her in like a needy child, she didn't know how she'd face him.

"Good gravy," she muttered, sinking down on the chair and holding her head in her hands. "I sure enough stepped in it this time."

The last person she wanted to see her as weak was Braxton Douglas. In the weeks she'd been at Bramble Hall, she'd come to admire him for his strength and kindness, as well as his gentleness.

What would he think of her now? Now that he knew she was an emotional wreck, resentful of the fear-driven decisions her mother had made.

Only Dacey didn't feel like a wreck. She didn't even feel as resentful of her mother.

Perhaps she'd needed to release all the emotions she'd bottled up for so long so she could move forward into her future, whatever it held.

Regret that Braxton happened to be the one present when her tears spilled all over added haste to her actions as she dressed.

On quiet feet, she made her way down the stairs to the kitchen where she begged Cook to give her two biscuits spread with a thick layer of apple butter. She planned to sneak outside before the rest of the house awakened. Eventually, she'd have to face Braxton, but she hoped to put it off until dinner.

With the biscuits in one hand and a tin cup of coffee in the other, she rushed out the back door. She stood on the step as the mere hint of a glorious sunrise began to lighten the sky. The edge of the cup brushed her lip as a warm hand settled on her back, making her squeal and jump, spilling coffee down the front of her skirt.

"Botheration!" she fumed, turning around to look into Braxton's smiling face. In the dim light, she could still see humor flickering in his mesmerizing gray eyes.

He smirked and took the cup from her, offering her a snowy white handkerchief. She handed him her biscuits then wiped her hand and brushed at her skirt.

"If you planned to scare the dickens out of me, you succeeded, Brax. What in thunderation did you do that for?"

Braxton smiled, biting into one of the biscuits before replying.

"I saw you come outside and wanted to make sure you were well after last night."

In the cool morning air, the warmth of his breath turned into white, feathery plumes as he spoke. His deep voice did strange things to Dacey's insides.

A shiver that had nothing to do with the cold and everything to do with Braxton coursed through her, making her tremble.

Braxton noticed and assumed she was chilled. He tossed the biscuits to one of the dogs lounging on the porch and took Dacey's arm in his, pulling her back inside the warmth of the house.

"Where's your coat? Why don't you have on your gloves? Are you trying to take ill?" He peppered her with questions as they walked through the kitchen. He thumped the empty tin cup on a counter as they passed through then urged Dacey up the back stairs to the third floor. "What were you thinking? Do you always run around in the cold without adequate covering?"

"Just hold your horses, buster." Dacey stopped partway up the steps and glared at him, fisting her hands on her hips. "I leave my chore coat at the horse barn, my gloves are in my pocket, and if I take ill it's because you made me soak my skirt with coffee. Since I rarely get sick, I ain't gonna worry about it. And I planned to eat those biscuits, you know. They had apple butter on them."

Braxton held back a smirk as she took two more steps upward until she stood on eye level with him.

"While you've got me riled up, I reckon I better speak my piece." She drew in a deep breath and continued. "I was heading to the barn early so I wouldn't have to apologize to you first thing this morning, but it looks like I get to do it anyway. I reckon that's a good lesson learned, to not put off something unpleasant just because I don't want to face it." A long sigh escaped her and she looked to Braxton with an expression of sincere regret. "I'm sorry about last night, Brax. I didn't mean to cry all over you like some simpering fool. And I appreciate you staying with me until I fell asleep. In addition, I'm sorry for losing my temper a minute ago. You just…"

"Scared you spitless?" Braxton teased. His index finger traced along the smooth line of her jaw and over the sweet arch of her cheek. "Apology accepted, Dacey, although you shouldn't be concerned about last night. I think you've needed to do that for a while and I'm glad I was there."

Frightened by the flames flickering in his eyes as he studied her, she nodded her head in agreement. Before she threw her arms around his neck and discovered how wonderful it would be to kiss his inviting lips, she spun around and raced the rest of the way up the stairs.

"I'll see you at breakfast," she called over her shoulder before disappearing down the hall.

Braxton rolled his eyes heavenward, wondering how long he could keep his desire to kiss Dacey, to own her completely, under control.

~~*~~

"Oh, Ernie. How wonderful to see you." Beatrice greeted Ernie Howell as he made a delivery to the kitchen. She'd been watching for his arrival, excited to implement the next phase of her plan to open Braxton's eyes to the treasure he had in Dacey, if he'd just accept her.

"It is providential I happened to catch you this afternoon," Beatrice gushed, guiding a befuddled Ernie down the hall toward the blue parlor where Dacey worked with her tutor.

"It is, ma'am?" Ernie asked, clearly confused.

"It most certainly is, young man. Miss Butler is in need of a dance partner and here you are."

"Miss Butler?" Ernie warmed to the idea of dancing with the lovely Dacey. Although she'd been polite to him, she hadn't appeared won over by his good looks or charm. Most women had a hard time resisting him, but Dacey seemed to be an exception.

With a little effort on his part, he was sure he could convince her to share at least a few kisses.

"I'd be happy to help Miss Butler," he said, smiling at Mrs. Douglas. She led the way into a large room where a harried little man attempted to instruct Dacey in the fine art of dancing the polka.

Ernie immediately took Dacey's hand in his and pulled her into the lively dance as the surprised tutor watched.

Beatrice worked to keep from rubbing her hands together in glee as her plans fell into place.

While the couple danced, Beatrice sent Caroline to round up a few of the house staff so they could practice a Virginia reel.

No doubt, Dacey had never even seen one and it would require more than two people to illustrate the dance.

Caroline soon returned with Cornelia and a housemaid, along with the butler, one of the kitchen helpers, and two of the gardeners.

When the polka ended, they all took their places as the tutor explained the Virginia reel to Dacey.

Partnered with George, Beatrice watched as the others stepped into line. As they went through the steps, she kept one eye on Dacey and the other on the door, waiting for Braxton to appear.

At the end of the dance, Beatrice insisted they practice again. As she spun around, she caught sight of her son's frown as he stood just inside the room, watching Ernie's every move as he guided Dacey through the steps.

"Thank you all for your wonderful assistance," Beatrice said as the staff dispersed to return to their work. She looked to the tutor. "Doesn't she need to practice the waltz?"

"Yes, ma'am, most certainly. It is nearly impossible to tutor her and dance at the same time. If Mr. Howell would like to assist, it would…"

"Not be necessary for him to stay." Braxton strode across the room until he stood next to Dacey.

Ernie had yet to relinquish his hold on her hand. At Braxton's arrival, he'd tightened his grip and dared to place a possessive hand at Dacey's waist.

Braxton's fist unknowingly clenched at his side. He wanted to pop Ernie in the nose, but somehow refrained from surrendering to the primitive urge.

"I have a few moments of free time. I'll help Miss Butler with her dancing lessons. I'm sure Mr. Howell has other deliveries to make. We've detained him long enough." Braxton took Dacey's free hand in his and gave it a gentle tug.

Rather than admit defeat and leave, Ernie yanked on her hand, pulling her closer to him. Braxton shot Ernie a warning glare and again tugged on Dacey's hand.

Fed up with the childish behavior of both men, Dacey jerked her hands free and stepped away from them.

"I believe I've danced all I care to today," she said, giving Beatrice a pleading look.

"Very well, darling." Beatrice settled an arm around her shoulders and gave her an indulgent smile. "Ernie, we appreciate your help. Let me walk you to the kitchen."

Before the young man could protest, Beatrice looped her hand around his arm and rushed him out of the room.

Braxton stared at Dacey, wondering what she'd do if he took her in his arms and danced with her. The sudden desire to glide her across the floor drove him to nod to the tutor. The man began playing a waltz on the phonograph.

With no time to protest, she found herself swept into the dance with Braxton's arm around her. A scent that put her in mind of spicy autumn air and rich leather invaded her senses.

Lost in the splendor of being held in his arms, of being near him, she tipped back her head and looked into his face. She took in his wavy, unkempt hair. No doubt, he'd forked his fingers through it many times already that day. He wore a gray shirt and waistcoat that accented the color of his eyes with black riding breeches tucked into knee-high black boots.

Braxton Douglas cut quite a dashing figure, one that nearly stole her breath away.

Although Dacey knew very little about dancing or men, she decided she could happily spend hours waltzing with Braxton. Not only was he a wonderful dancer, but he patiently instructed her without making her feel silly or stupid.

When the song ended, Braxton looked to the tutor. The man nodded and played it again. By the third time they danced to the song, Dacey had mastered the steps.

The tutor excused himself, mindful of the charged atmosphere in the room as Braxton continued to dance with Dacey long after the music had stopped.

Ever so slowly, he applied slight pressure to her waist and she stepped closer to him, head swimming while her limbs grew languid.

"Braxton," she whispered on a plea, leaning her forehead against his solid chest.

"What do you need, honey?" he asked in a husky rumble against her hair.

Dacey closed her eyes and breathed in his scent, let his warmth penetrate clear down to her soul as their movements stilled and she rested in the circle of his arms.

What did she need?

You.

Unable to verbalize her longing, the only thing she needed or wanted was Braxton. Nothing else mattered. No one else existed to her in that moment.

Only him.

His arms tightened around her. "Dacey Jo?"

"Hmm?"

"Look at me," he ordered. She obeyed, tipping back her head to stare at him.

He smiled and lowered his head toward hers.

She held her breath, anticipating the moment their lips would connect. Unlike the other day beneath the copper leaves of the weeping beech tree, Dacey wouldn't run away. She ached to taste his kiss.

Keen disappointment settled over her when Beatrice breezed into the room with the tutor, startling them both.

Dacey stepped away from Braxton while he muttered darkly under his breath.

"Darling, I believe you've almost mastered all the dance steps. You'll be the belle of the ball next week," Beatrice said as she took Dacey's hand and led her from the room.

Dacey paused for a moment in the doorway and glanced back at Braxton before following his mother down the hall.

Frustrated, he scowled at the tutor and strode from the room, intent on saddling a horse. A long ride would help clear his head and cool the fever Dacey had innocently stirred.

In the weeks since her arrival, he'd become quite experienced at banking the fires she unwittingly kindled in him.

Chapter Nine

"I'm going to be ill," Dacey moaned, pressing cool hands to her flushed cheeks.

The entire plantation had been in a fuss the past several days, preparing for the famed Harvest Ball.

Apparently, Beatrice and Daniel had hosted the dance every November for the past twenty years. Uppity members of society from all around the area attended the ball, dubbed the event of the season. In addition, the Douglas family invited anyone in town who wanted to attend.

Dacey had jumped into the preparations, helping festoon the ballroom with colorful leaves, pumpkins and gilded branches. Fashioning decorations and sampling the goodies the kitchen created for the event had been great fun.

Nevertheless, the idea of donning the dress Beatrice had ordered for her and attending the event left her ill at ease and terrified of making some unforgivable blunder.

Her stomach churned as her face paled.

"You'll be fine," Cornelia said, adjusting the satin ruffle on Dacey's left shoulder. "You look stunning."

Dacey smiled at her friend in the reflection of the mirror's glass. "More like a mule in a thoroughbred's barn, but it's kind of you to say otherwise."

Cornelia grinned and fluffed the tendrils of hair she'd left hanging around Dacey's face. "I wouldn't say it if I didn't mean it. You'll be the most beautiful girl at the ball and if Braxton doesn't notice, he's not half as smart as we all think."

"I ain't got..." Dacey sighed and rolled her eyes. "I mean, I do not possess a single chance with a man such as Braxton Douglas. He's made it abundantly clear he has no interest in taking a bride. When he could have a rich, beautiful girl of his standing, why on earth would he even look my direction?"

"Because you make him laugh and smile," Cornelia said, helping Dacey tug on the long satin gloves that reached her upper arms.

"Mercy, I feel like a trussed up turkey. Between the corset and these confounded petticoats, I've been properly caged and tied."

Giggles erupted out of Cornelia but she quickly subdued them when a knock sounded at the door. Beatrice's maid Caroline stepped into the room.

"Oh, Miss Butler," Caroline said, smiling as she took her in from the curls piled on her head to the embroidered toes of her shoes. "You are sure to turn heads this evening."

"I reckon that's better than turning stomachs," Dacey teased, making both women laugh. "What can we do for you, Caroline?"

"Mrs. Douglas asked me to check on you. She and Mr. Douglas just went down to the ballroom." Caroline hovered in the doorway, offering Dacey an encouraging nod. "When you are ready, she said for you to venture downstairs."

"Might as well go right now because if I stay up here thinking on how much I don't want to do this, I really will be sick."

Cornelia patted her back and walked with her to the door. "Don't worry, Dacey. Just smile and be yourself."

Dacey tapped Cornelia's arm with the fan she held in her hand. "I know for certain that will get me into trouble."

"Oh, don't let any of them intimidate you, Miss Butler," Caroline said as the three of them stepped into the hall. "Those stuffy ol' gossips could use a fresh breeze like you to rustle their skirts… or bloomers."

Cornelia gaped at Caroline before all three of them giggled. The two maids walked her down the hallway and along a corridor to another hallway that eventually took them to the stairs near the ballroom.

"I appreciate you two cheering me up. Wish me luck and send up a prayer that I don't humiliate the family this evening." Dacey took a deep breath and started down the curved staircase.

Carefully focused on her descent, she didn't notice anyone at the bottom until a hand touched her elbow and she glanced up into Braxton's smiling face.

He leaned down, his whispered words stirring the curls near her ear. "I think you just stole my breath away, Dacey Jo. You look beautiful."

She blushed and nervously slipped the cord of her fan over her wrist.

Sensing her discomfort, Braxton placed a hand to her waist and gave it a slight squeeze. "I meant every word, honey. You're the prettiest girl here this evening." In fact, Braxton didn't know how he'd keep his wits about him with Dacey appearing so enchanting.

The gown his mother ordered for her fit to perfection and the deep teal color matched her alluring eyes while enhancing the deep auburn shade of her hair.

Dacey Butler might be a simple girl from a ranch out west, but she was the loveliest creature Braxton could ever recall seeing. Yet far more than her outward appearance captured his interest. A large part of the attraction he experienced came from how happy and light his heart felt in her presence.

Fully aware of the wolves dressed in expensive clothing inside the ballroom, Braxton planned to keep Dacey near his side throughout the evening.

A few of his close friends had met her and been thoroughly charmed. The rest of his crowd, though, would do their best to eat her alive, particularly some of the girls he'd spurned.

Concerned that Dacey enjoy her evening, Braxton had taken the liberty of filling her dance card. Although he wanted to claim every dance, he added the names of his friends, his father, and a few others he could trust to treat the girl kindly.

His mother had also promised to keep an eye on her. Between the two of them, he hoped she would make it through the evening unhurt.

"Are you ready to go in?" Braxton asked as they stood outside the ballroom door.

Entranced by the sight of the room, filled with a rainbow of colors from the autumn decorations to the women in gowns of every hue imaginable, Dacey merely nodded her head.

Crystal chandeliers sparkled overhead while soft lights glowed from wall sconces. Tables placed around the edges of the room held centerpieces of gold, orange, burgundy, and red leaves and flowers with white candles.

The overall effect was spectacular.

"Oh, Brax. It looks so..." She struggled to find a word to do the vision before her justice. "Magical."

He chuckled and nudged her forward. "Well, you helped make it that way. Mother said they'd never have finished the decorations if you hadn't taken charge of gathering leaves and branches.

"Shoot. That was easy. Cornelia and the others made it all look so pretty."

Braxton caught his mother's eye and the woman hurried their direction as they entered the ballroom. "Be that as it may, we couldn't have done this without you."

Dacey smiled as Beatrice wrapped her in a warm hug then kissed her cheek.

"Both of you look just splendid," Beatrice said, patting Braxton's cheek as she slipped her arm around Dacey's waist. "Dacey, darling, you must meet my dear friends. They live over near Knoxville and come every year for the ball. Olivia and I were childhood playmates and…"

Dacey glanced over her shoulder at Braxton as his mother led her off to meet her friends. He winked at her and a becoming pink blush highlighted her cheeks.

Lost in watching her walk away, he failed to notice the woman sidling up next to him until she wrapped her hand around his arm.

"Braxton, I thought she'd never leave you alone. Who is that odd creature?"

Barely suppressing an annoyed sigh, he skillfully removed his arm from her grasp and took a step away from Miranda, the girl he'd once been stupid enough to court for a very brief, unpleasant time.

She hadn't taken it well when he'd told her he no longer wanted to see her. In fact, she'd screamed, slapped his face, and behaved like an enraged harridan. She'd sent him notes, followed him if he set foot in town, and begged him to reconsider. As a final effort to control him, she'd concocted a lie that he'd compromised her. Since she'd tried that ploy before, no one believed her outlandish claims.

Braxton had begged his mother to leave Miranda and her family off the guest list for the ball, but she insisted it would be unforgivably rude to leave them out.

He should have known the conniving woman would immediately notice Dacey.

"That beautiful, intelligent girl is a friend of the family, Miss Beaudry." Braxton overlooked the sneer on Miranda's face as she glared at Dacey.

"Why is she here?"

Braxton looked around for a means of escape. He spied Ernie Howell heading Dacey's direction. Hastily, he took Miranda's elbow in his hand, propelling her forward. "She's visiting through the holidays. Miss Butler and Mother are quite close."

"And what about you and Miss Butler?" Miranda asked with malice in her tone.

Rather than answer, Braxton intercepted Ernie and shoved Miranda forward. "Ernie, my friend, you know Miss Beaudry, don't you? Would you be so kind as to escort her over to the punch table? Since her mouth runs constantly, I'm afraid she'll soon become quite parched."

Indignant, Miranda huffed as Ernie grinned and turned her toward the punch table.

A slap on his back drew Braxton's gaze to his good friend, Jackson Hollis.

Jackson chuckled as he shook his head. "That was a particularly fitting remark, but I don't know that it's in your best interest to provoke Miss Beaudry. She's already been acting like a scorned tempest since that debacle back in the spring. Antagonizing her this evening will not end well."

"I know it, Jack, but that woman is such a..." Braxton stopped himself before he said something he shouldn't. "Anyway, Ernie will keep her entertained this evening and hopefully she'll keep him too busy to bother Dacey."

Jack followed Braxton's gaze to where Beatrice introduced Dacey to a group of older women. "She's a sweet, lovely young thing, Brax. What are you going to do with her?"

Braxton frowned at his friend. "Do with her? I'm not going to do anything with her. And she isn't all that young. She'll be twenty-three in January."

"Sounds to me like she's ripe for the picking," Jackson said, grinning at his boyhood chum. "In light of your disinterest in the matter of winning her heart, I suppose you won't mind if I give it a go."

Jackson took a step Dacey's direction before Braxton placed a hand on his arm, pulling him to a stop.

"That's enough of your nonsense," Braxton cautioned.

Jackson laughed and thumped Braxton on the back again. "Even if you won't acknowledge your feelings, you're entirely gone for the girl, my friend. You might as well surrender to the inevitable and admit it."

"I'm not admitting to anything." Braxton glowered at a young man who approached Dacey with a cup of punch. "I'll talk to you later, Jack. Enjoy your evening."

Without another word, he hustled across the ballroom to thwart any plans the young man might have held about charming her.

Later, after they'd enjoyed a delicious feast, the first notes of music floated across the ballroom, beckoning dancers to the floor.

"Shall we?" Braxton asked, leaning close to Dacey from his seat beside her at a table.

"Are you sure I can't just sit back and watch?" Dacey asked as Braxton stood then held a hand out to her.

"Positive. Mother would be terribly disappointed if you didn't join in the fun, especially after all those hours you spent with the tutor." Braxton led her out to the dance floor and positioned his hands to lead her in the waltz.

At first, Dacey appeared stiff and tense. As the music engrossed her and she watched the other dancers in their formal attire, eventually she relaxed.

"Oh, Braxton, isn't her dress something?" Dacey whispered as one of his mother's friends twirled past them. "It looks like the stars fell out of the sky and latched right onto her gown."

Braxton grinned. "Those are rhinestones. Blue velvet certainly sets them off." He nodded in the direction of the woman wearing the sparkling gown. "Mrs. Wilkins is one of mother's closest friends. As a young lad, she'd bring me sassafras drops when she came to visit."

Dacey smiled. "That was kind of her."

The look he gave Dacey held a bit of repugnance. "I love all types of sweets, but sassafras drops taste like medicine to me. For years, I thought she didn't like me and brought them as a form of punishment. Mother always made me thank her and eat one to be polite. It was horrid."

Laughter spilled out of Dacey, drawing the gazes of nearby dancers their direction. Embarrassed by the attention, she immediately quieted.

"Laugh all you want, honey. No one cares. They're just admiring the delightful woman I'm fortunate enough to escort this evening."

"Braxton, you shouldn't tell fibs."

He affected a wounded look. "That cuts me to the quick, Miss Butler. How rude to imply I might utter an untruth."

A grin lifted the corners of her mouth as she saw the mirth in his eyes and the teasing in his smile. "You've uttered plenty of untruths since I've been here, starting with telling me opossum are really cuddly pets that live in the woods. I nearly lost a finger when I picked up the one that was out by the smoke house."

"You had on gloves. Besides, I was more worried about the poor rodent when you tossed it so indignantly into the shrubbery."

"Well, we don't have them where I grew up. In my opinion, they look like a badger got a little too friendly with a demented rat and created hideous offspring."

Braxton threw back his head and laughed as he spun Dacey around the dance floor. Several indulgent glances turned their way, except for Miranda Beaudry and her friends. They huddled in a corner, tossing frosty glares his direction.

When the waltz finished, Braxton hesitated to release Dacey to her next dance partner. Since it was his father, though, he felt somewhat assured she'd be in good hands.

Braxton danced with his mother, then some of her friends while Dacey went from one dance partner to the next.

However, the moment Ernie Howell cut in, Braxton saw Dacey glancing around for him, sending a silent plea for help.

Unable to extricate himself from his current dance partner without causing a scene, Braxton caught Jackson's eye as he stood with a group of young men. He tipped his head Dacey's direction. Jackson took the unspoken cue.

Quickly striding across the room, he tapped Ernie on the shoulder and cut in, sweeping Dacey into a lively polka.

As the evening progressed, Braxton let down his guard, pleased to see most everyone welcomed Dacey with open arms.

Although both he and Beatrice encouraged her to be herself, she'd been very careful about her speech and manners. It had to be as wearing on her nerves as it had been on his, watching her hold part of herself back for fear of making a social misstep.

Tired of the noise around him, Braxton opened a side door and strode out onto the balcony.

In the light spilling from the ballroom and the moon overhead, he noticed a figure leaning against the railing in the shadows.

"I'm sorry, I didn't mean to intrude." He turned to go, but the voice that carried through the darkness made him stop.

"You ain't bothering me, buster."

He smiled and stepped behind Dacey, placing a warm hand on her back. "What are you doing out here, honey? You'll catch a chill without a coat."

"It's hotter than blazes in there and I needed a moment of quiet and some fresh air." Dacey looked at him over her shoulder and straightened. "I hope that's okay."

Braxton nodded and looked out at the peaceful night. He moved beside her, resting his elbows on the railing. "It's perfectly fine. That's the reason I escaped out here for a few moments."

"We're quite a pair, ain't we?" Dacey teased, playfully bumping his arm with hers.

Although her words were meant in fun, Braxton took them to heart. He and Dacey were a well-suited pair.

The fact they came from entirely different worlds didn't matter to him. Dacey shared his sense of humor, his obsession for horses, and they'd even read many of the same books. Stubborn, opinionated, hard working, and loyal were traits they had in common.

When he was with her, he felt unconquerable, as if he could do anything in the world. She made him laugh and think, dream and feel.

More than anything, he wanted her always to be a part of his life. Without giving a thought to his actions, he gathered her in his arms, drawing her against his chest.

"Dacey?"

"Yes?" she whispered, gazing up at him in the muted light. She'd imagined his kiss so many times, she hesitated to believe it might actually happen. The entire evening had been a wonderful dream. The only thing that would make it better was for Braxton to press his lips to hers.

"You are the most beautiful woman I've ever seen, Dacey Jo Butler." His head lowered toward hers, but he stopped when his mouth was a breath of space away from hers. "I want to kiss you in the worst way."

In impatient agony, she smiled. "What are you waitin' on, buster?"

Softly, his mouth brushed over hers. Her hands trailed up his arms and curled around the back of his neck.

He wrapped both arms around her, lifting her off her feet as the kiss went from tender and sweet to overflowing with decadent passion.

Completely captivated, his lips teased and coaxed hers until they both were breathless.

He started to lift his head, to apologize for his fervent attention to her mouth, but she bracketed his face with her hands and engaged him in a kiss that kicked every bit of his sense right out of his head.

Time stopped as their lips blended again and again until a noise at the doorway made her gasp. Braxton reluctantly set her back on her feet.

Jackson cleared his throat to hide a chuckle. "Your mother is looking for you, Brax. She was concerned because she couldn't find Dacey. I see you've got everything under control." Jackson turned around, still amused. "I think I'll go find myself a cup of punch."

"Punch. That's a great idea," Braxton said, desperate for anything to clear his thoughts. He took Dacey's hand in his, prepared to lead her back into the ballroom.

She squeezed his fingers, but didn't follow when he moved toward the door.

"Do you mind if I stay out here just a little while longer?"

He stepped close and brushed his thumb across her just-kissed lips. "Not at all, honey. Just don't tarry too long. The temperature is dropping and I don't want you to catch a chill."

"I won't." Dacey watched him return inside the ballroom. She needed a moment alone to absorb the notion that Braxton Douglas had just kissed her more thoroughly and completely than she ever dared imagine.

Giddy with pure bliss, she turned to gaze into the night. A sense of rightness, of being where she belonged filled her as she lifted her face up to the clear sky filled with stars.

About to fly apart from the joy filling her heart, Dacey wrapped her arms around her middle and sighed contentedly.

"He doesn't really love you, you know. You're just another conquest to Braxton."

Dacey spun around, shocked by the words of the woman standing behind her. She could make out blond hair and a dazzling yellow gown that sparkled in the light from the ballroom. She vaguely remembered Beatrice introducing the woman as Miss Beaudry with a whispered warning that Miranda's tongue was sharp on both sides and prone to cutting remarks.

Rather than acknowledge the woman, Dacey hurried past her to return inside. The girl grabbed her arm in a fierce hold, stopping her progress.

"I'm only trying to help you, Miss Butler," the woman said in a syrupy voice. "Braxton has quite a reputation of pursuing girls until they give him what he wants. When he's satisfied, he moves on, leaving a trail of broken hearts in his wake."

Hurt, Dacey yanked her arm from the girl's grasp. "Braxton isn't like that. Not at all. He's kind and generous and…"

"Charming and sweet, plying you with praise and making you feel like the most important person in the world." Miranda twirled the fan on her wrist around and around before giving Dacey a sympathetic look. "It's all an act, Miss Butler. The only thing Braxton wants is to, well... it's not something to discuss in polite company. But it all starts with a kiss under the stars."

Caught off guard by the fact Miranda knew he'd kissed her, doubts began to assail Dacey. What if the woman spoke the truth? What if Braxton didn't care about her and was just using her as a means to an end that would leave her devastated?

Miranda looped her hand around Dacey's arm, moving closer to the ballroom door. "Don't feel badly, Miss Butler. You aren't the first girl to be taken in by Braxton's good looks and silver tongue. Nor shall you be the last. Really, it's a pity his mother indulged him to the point that he's a..." Miranda leaned close and dropped her voice to a whisper, "seducer."

Dacey gave her a shocked look of disbelief as they entered the ballroom.

"It's true, dear. If you need more proof, just ask around. You'll find any number of girls who've barely escaped his amorous clutches," Miranda said, tilting her head toward a group of nearby young women. "We must protect each other from a beast like Braxton."

Numb, Dacey excused herself. She made it to the punch table and accepted a cup of the cold, fruity drink from one of the staff.

After emptying the cup, she turned and watched Braxton dancing with a tall, dark-haired woman.

The two of them appeared quite fond of each other. Pangs of jealousy pricked Dacey when Braxton leaned closer and said something that made them both laugh.

As the dance ended, he settled his hand on the woman's waist and guided her off the dance floor.

Maybe the vile words Miranda Beaudry spoke were true. Maybe Braxton planned to take what he could from her then move on to his next victim. If he was such a ruthless cad, it would explain why he'd never wed.

Dacey stared as a housemaid approached the woman and Braxton carrying a little boy who looked exactly like him.

Braxton took the boy and tossed him into the air, making him smile. He carried the youngster over to where Beatrice chatted with several older women. She took the child and kissed his cheek before the dark-haired woman lifted the boy in her arms and tenderly held him as she left the room.

"I see you noticed Braxton's son," Miranda said from beside Dacey.

"Son?" Dacey squeaked, not ready to believe what she'd seen.

"Oh, I imagine there's more than that one," Miranda said, making the two girls with her nod in agreement.

Dacey found it impossible to breathe. The air in the ballroom suddenly seemed stifling. Drawing on the last shred of dignity she possessed, she nodded to the women beside her. "Please excuse me Miss Beaudry, Miss Cedric, Miss Cash. Enjoy your evening."

With as much decorum as she could muster, Dacey strode from the ballroom with her head high, shoulders back, and her heart breaking into a million little pieces.

Unable to remember how to make it back to the main part of the house through the maze of halls and turns, she hurried down the porch steps and across the lawn to the front door. Upon entering, she raced up the stairs to her room and collapsed on her bed in tears.

Even Cornelia's comforting hand on her back and the maid's genuine concern couldn't get her to stop crying long enough to explain.

"Please, Cornelia. Just help me get out of this wretched dress."

Once Cornelia helped her remove the finery, Dacey gave her a hug then pushed her toward the door. "Please, Corny, leave me alone. Just leave me be."

Cornelia left the room, but remained in the hall, worried for her distraught friend.

Chapter Ten

"Have you seen Dacey?" Braxton asked Jackson as he surveyed the ballroom.

He thought he'd seen Miranda talking to her earlier, but by the time he made it to the punch table, both women had disappeared. Given the opportunity, he had no doubt Miranda would release her venomous tongue on Dacey.

"I haven't seen her for about an hour, Brax. Not since I caught the two of you out on the balcony." Jackson chuckled. "For a moment, you looked like you might strike a blow to my jaw when I unknowingly interrupted your um... interlude."

Braxton scowled at him and continued studying the crowd, hoping for a glance of a teal satin gown and auburn curls.

"Come on, Brax." Jackson clapped a hand on his shoulder. "Why don't you just admit the truth."

"The truth?" Braxton asked, distracted that he still hadn't located Dacey.

"Yes, the truth. You can pretend all you like that she doesn't matter to you, but you're in love with Dacey Butler. Anyone with eyes in their head can see you've fallen for the girl." Braxton's look of surprise brought another round of chuckles from his friend. "Everyone is talking about the sparks flying between the two of you when you get within arm's length of each other."

"Is that so?" Braxton walked toward his mother.

"It's a fact, my friend." Jackson grinned and asked a pretty brown-haired girl for a dance while Braxton approached Beatrice and a group of her friends.

Politely, he waited for a lull in the conversation before touching his mother's arm.

"Oh, hello, dear. Are you having fun?" Beatrice asked, affectionately patting his cheek.

"Not at the moment. I can't seem to locate Dacey." Braxton spoke quietly, bending down close to his mother's ear.

"Well, we must find her, then." Beatrice took his hand in hers and the two of them walked the length and breadth of the ballroom, but still couldn't find Dacey.

"Perhaps she didn't feel well or became weary. I'll ask Caroline to check with Cornelia." Beatrice turned to summon her maid, but Braxton stopped her.

"I'll go check myself, Mother. She was warm earlier. Maybe she took ill and didn't want to worry us."

"I certainly hope she's well, Brax. I have such a fun day planned tomorrow now that Charlotte and Billy are here."

"I'm sure she'll enjoy it. If you'll excuse me, I'll go back to the main wing and see if she's there. You know how she likes to sit in the library by the fire of an evening." Braxton kissed his mother's velvety cheek then rushed out of the ballroom and down the steps to the lawn. It was faster to run around the outside of the house than meander through the maze of hallways to reach the bedrooms on the third floor.

He raced inside the front door of the house and checked both the blue and gold parlors, but Dacey wasn't in either room. The library stood empty and she wasn't in the music room, so he rushed upstairs. He stopped short when he came upon Cornelia sitting outside Dacey's door, fretfully wringing her hands together.

"Cornelia? What's the matter? Where's Dacey?" he asked, noting the concern on the girl's face.

"I'm so glad you're here, Mr. Douglas. Dacey returned in tears a while ago and won't talk to me. She asked me to leave her alone, but she's been crying the whole time." Cornelia pointed to the door where the soft sound of sobs was barely audible in the hall.

"You go on and rest. I'll take care of her." Braxton smiled at the young woman then opened Dacey's door.

"Dacey?" He stepped inside the room and noticed her prone position on the bed with her face pressed into a pillow while her hair tumbled around her shoulders and down her back. The light from the bedside lamp created valleys of dark red and peaks of gold in the tresses. His hands ached to run through the silky curls. "Are you unwell?"

She lifted her tear-streaked face and glared at him. "Leave me alone, Braxton Douglas. I never want to speak to you again."

"What's wrong, honey?"

Quickly pushing herself upright, she glared at him and used the sleeve of her nightgown to swipe at her tears. "Don't you honey me, you... you... cad."

Confused by her anger and name-calling, he tried to recall something he'd done to upset her. Unable to think of little else beyond the fantastical kisses they'd shared on the balcony, he couldn't come up with anything.

Suddenly, he wondered if Miranda had spoken to her, uttered some untruth that wounded her. "Did someone say something to upset you?" He strode to the bed in a few long strides and placed a hand on her shoulder. "If you spoke with..."

As though his touch pained her, she winced. With a rough jerk away from him, she rolled off the side of the bed and scrambled to her feet.

"Get out!" She jabbed a finger toward the door. "Get out of my room and leave me be!"

Afraid she might grow hysterical in her current state of distress, Braxton quietly backed out the door and closed it. He turned around to find Cornelia still waiting in the hall.

"Is there anything I can do to help, sir?" Cornelia asked.

Braxton shook his head. "As you probably heard, she won't have anything to do with me either." He sighed and ran a hand though his hair, staring at the closed bedroom door. Finally, he turned back to Cornelia. "She didn't say anything to you when she returned?"

"No, sir. I helped her change then she asked me to leave her alone. I didn't know what to do. She seems so unlike herself." Cornelia continued wringing her hands together.

"I suppose for now we should abide by her wishes." Braxton offered the faithful little maid an encouraging smile. "Go on and get some rest, Cornelia. I'm sure things will be back to normal in the morning."

At least Braxton prayed they would.

~~*~~

"Where's Dacey?" Beatrice asked as she breezed into the breakfast room. A dark-haired child who looked like a miniature version of Braxton rode on her hip.

"I haven't seen her yet this morning," Braxton said, rising to his feet and tickling the boy beneath his chin. "She wasn't in her room and Cornelia said she mentioned something about going out to work with the horses. You know she often does that, so maybe all is well this morning."

Although Braxton tried to convince the others, the gnawing anxiety in his gut warned him the storm with Dacey had not fully passed.

Determined to put on a good face, he took the little one from his mother and tossed him in the air. "And how are you today, Billy? Are you excited to spend the day with your grandmother?"

"Yes, sir." Billy nodded his head and looked at Braxton with stormy gray eyes so like his. "Will you come, too?"

"I'll join you later, but I have some things I must attend to first." Braxton set the child on a chair beside him and pulled it close to his. He smiled at the boy's mother as she took a seat across the table from him. "You're looking lovely this morning, Charlotte."

"Thank you, Brax. I appreciate the compliment." The beautiful woman winked at him. "Please, sugar, won't you join us? It's been so long since we've had a good visit."

"I really must see to a few matters, but I'll do my best to join you this afternoon," Braxton said. He buttered a piece of toast for Billy and set it on his plate. Affectionately, he ruffled the child's hair before filling his own plate.

Charlotte offered him a becoming pout as she stirred sugar into her tea. "We hardly see you, Braxton. Billy and I miss spending time with you."

"I know, and for that I'm sorry. I really will try to get to Greenville with more frequency in the future."

From her hiding spot in the hall, Dacey watched as Braxton gave the woman named Charlotte a tender glance across the table. An undeniable look of pure love was on his face as he smiled at the child.

Tears stung her eyes as she backed away from the door and ran upstairs.

Arising early that morning, she thought perhaps she had overreacted the previous evening.

After going out to check on the horses and riding one of her favorites, she decided to give Braxton a chance to explain what Miranda had said, especially about him having a son.

She'd hurried to wash and change before joining the family in the breakfast room. The sight of Braxton tending to the child as he conversed with the dark-haired woman he'd been with last night caused her to hide just outside the door.

Swiftly concluding she hadn't overreacted, she hastened to her room and began stuffing her belongings into the trunk on the floor of the closet. As she packed, she formulated a plan.

With Braxton's mistress and son there, she couldn't stay. She wouldn't stay.

No one with a speck of sense or an ounce of pride would want to reside under the same roof as a man like that.

Thoughts of all his kindnesses, of all the entire family had done to make her feel welcome and loved poked at her heart, but she shoved the memories aside.

Fury added speed to her movements as she filled her valise with a change of clothes and her most necessary items.

Careful not to take anything Beatrice or Braxton had given her, she glanced around the room and made sure she hadn't left anything of hers behind.

Resolute, she sat at the writing desk. She penned a note to Beatrice, another to Cornelia, then copied a forwarding address from a slip of paper she'd tucked into her coat pocket.

Three men interested in purchasing horses from Braxton had stopped by the previous week while Dacey worked with one of the colts in a pen near the barn.

One of the men had been quite taken with her ability and offered her a position on his horse farm if she ever needed one.

As Dacey once again found herself without a place to call home, she decided to take him up on the offer. If she could get into town, she'd send him a telegram then purchase a train ticket to his farm near Hendersonville. Cornelia would see that her trunk arrived at the farm.

Dacey opened her reticule and counted out the exact amount she thought it would take to send the trunk. She placed the money with the address on top of the trunk. Carefully setting her reticule inside her valise, she buckled the top closed.

Rather than risk anyone noticing her leaving, she stepped onto the balcony and surveyed the lawn below. No one was in sight, so she dropped her valise into the shrubs two stories down. She'd fish it out later when she was ready to leave.

Back inside the warmth of her room, Dacey experienced a moment of regret. She'd never had such a fine room, especially one with a bathroom. She'd miss the conveniences Bramble Hall offered, but most of all she'd miss the people.

Cornelia and Caroline were her friends.

Beatrice, and even Daniel, had become like parents to her.

Her heart skipped a beat as she thought about Braxton. Oh, how she loved him, loved everything about him.

And that was why she had to leave, immediately.

If she didn't, she might be the next girl to succumb to his considerable charms. No matter how bad things seemed at the present, they'd be far worse when he tired of her and sent her away.

No, she'd leave now while nothing was wounded except her broken heart and a little piece of her pride for not realizing his true character sooner.

Still, it was hard to reconcile the Braxton she'd come to know with the womanizing rake Miss Beaudry described.

Regardless, the proof of his actions sat at the breakfast table next to him.

Determined to move forward and not look back at the wonderful weeks she spent at Bramble Hall, Dacey studied her room one last time then walked out the door, shutting it behind her.

Quietly, she crept along the hall to the servant's stairs and made her way to the kitchen where she talked Cook into giving her bread slathered with apple butter.

That was one more thing she'd sorely miss. Although she'd never tasted apple butter before arriving in Asheville, it took no time at all for her develop a fondness for the autumn-flavored treat.

"The family is still eating breakfast, miss. You should join them," Cook said as she handed Dacey two slices of warm bread spread with a thick layer of apple butter.

"No. I want to get to work early this morning." Dacey smiled fondly at the cook. "Thank you for being so kind to me and for making such delicious food."

"You're most welcome, Miss Butler." Cook gave her a baffled glance. "Is there something..."

"Have a wonderful morning. I'll see you later." Impulsively, Dacey hugged the woman and hustled outside, munching on the bread as she hurried around the house and retrieved her valise from the bushes.

She kept to the shadows and crept toward the river. From riding horses all over the property with Braxton, she knew she could follow it then cut through the apple orchard to take a mile off her walk into town.

Although the sun shone overhead, it was cold out. By the time she reached town, her fingers felt numb even through her gloves.

The extra pair of socks she'd donned to keep her feet warm caused her boots to pinch her toes. Convinced she'd developed at least one blister, she didn't have time to worry about it as she headed directly to the train depot.

The station office was open, so she walked inside and smiled at Mr. Jones when he glanced up at her.

"Miss Butler. To what do I owe the pleasure of your visit this morning?" he asked, straightening the papers in front of him as he spoke.

Dacey almost giggled at the gesture that had to be a habit. She stepped up to the counter and gave him her most charming smile. "I need a ticket to Hendersonville, if you please, Mr. Jones."

"Round trip?" he asked.

"No, sir. A one-way ticket. I'm not sure how long I'll be there." Dacey glanced around, glad no one else was in the room. The fewer witnesses who saw her run away from Bramble Hall, the better.

Mr. Jones gave her a curious look. "Are you taking your trunk?"

"No, sir. Only my valise."

"I see," the man said cryptically. "And you want to leave on today's train. One ticket. To Hendersonville."

Dacey wanted to stamp her foot. Were all agents so reluctant to sell a potential passenger a ticket? On the other hand, did Mr. Jones suspect she was running away? Either way, it really wasn't any of his concern.

"There is a train heading there today, isn't there?" she asked.

"Yes, indeed. It will pull out of the station at a few minutes past noon."

Relieved she'd only have to wait a few hours, she smiled at him again. "Then I'd like one ticket to be on it when it leaves."

"Are you sure, Miss Butler? I thought you were staying at Bramble Hall. In fact, you were at the Harvest Ball last evening, weren't you? I thought I caught a glimpse of you dancing with young Mr. Douglas."

"Yes, I did dance with him and it was a grand ball. The grandest I've ever seen." Dacey realized if she didn't have a good reason to be on that train, Mr. Jones would refuse to sell her a ticket. "The Douglas family is still entertaining visiting guests, so I'm traveling to Hendersonville to meet with one of Braxton's horse buyers."

Word of Dacey's talent with horses and her work with them at Bramble Hall had spread quickly through town. Based on that, it wouldn't seem too far-fetched for her to discuss horse business with an out-of-town buyer.

At least she hoped it wouldn't.

While she was at it, Dacey hoped she wouldn't be condemned for stretching the truth. Everything she said was true, just not the implication that she was meeting with the buyer on behalf of Braxton.

Mr. Jones stared at her for a long moment before nodding his head then turning around to get her ticket.

"I also need to send a telegram."

He gave her the price for the ticket and telegram. She dug the funds from her reticule after digging it out of her valise. She removed the correct amount of money then hung the reticule from her wrist. With the train ticket safely tucked into her coat pocket, she glanced at the big clock on the wall.

"Mr. Jones, would you mind if I left my valise here until the train arrives? I have a few errands to attend to before I leave town."

"That's fine. Give it to me and I'll set it here behind the counter."

Dacey handed over her few precious belongings and thanked the man. "I'll be back before noon."

"See that you are, or you'll have a long walk to Hendersonville."

She grinned and sailed out the door.

As she meandered along the street, once again looking in store windows, she thought of how frightened and unsure she'd been when she'd first arrived in town.

Now, she felt plagued by similar feelings, compounded by the regret of leaving Beatrice without a spoken word of thanks or a proper goodbye. Thoughts of Braxton made tears sting her eyes.

Purposely she ignored the pain taking up residence inside her chest in place of her heart. Falling in love with Braxton taught her a valuable lesson. One she wouldn't forget or repeat.

When something seems too good to be true, it generally is.

Chapter Eleven

"Dacey! What a pleasant surprise!" Ellie Howell hurried around the counter to give her a hug as she entered the store. "What are you doing in town today?"

"Oh, I had a few errands to run."

"I'm so glad you stopped by the store. Will you stay for a cup of tea?" Ellie asked with a hopeful gleam in her eye.

"I'd love a cup of tea, if you have time."

"I do," Ellie said, pulling Dacey over to the table where she'd sat and eaten a sandwich the day she first arrived in town.

Melancholy feelings swept over her, but she did her best to hide them with a bright smile.

As Ellie took a seat beside her and poured a cup of tea, Dacey breathed in the fragrant steam, cradling the cup in her hands and relishing the warmth it provided. "So, Ellie, what did you think of the ball last night?"

"I think it was the best one yet. Did you see Mrs. Ralston? She had the gown with..."

Dacey hid her grin behind her teacup as Ellie spent the next hour discussing her favorite gowns, hairstyles, food, and decorations from the previous evening's festivities.

"Did you see my Ernie? Didn't he look handsome?" Ellie beamed with pride as she mentioned her son.

Dacey decided a horrible flaw existed in local mothers, enabling them to see only the good in their offspring. Everyone in town except Ellie knew Ernie Howell was lazy and conniving, out to break as many hearts as possible.

Evidently, people in Asheville knew the truth about Braxton Douglas, too, even if they chose to ignore it.

Determined not to think about him, Dacey smiled at Ellie. "Ernie did look quite handsome. I saw him dancing with Miranda Beaudry. They made quite a striking couple."

"Oh, gracious, I must have missed that. I hope he didn't take an interest in that girl. She's nothing but trouble."

"Why do you say that, Ellie?" Dacey asked, suddenly very interested in Ellie's opinions.

"She'd rather lie than tell the truth and she all but accused Braxton of compromising her virtue in a desperate attempt to force him into marriage." Ellie leaned closer and lowered her voice to a whisper. "Even if he had, which no one believes, Miranda used that particular ploy before. The first boy she accused ran away from home to escape the horrible rumors, none of which was true. He hasn't set foot in town since then, and that was five years ago."

Startled by this revelation, Dacey began to wonder if perhaps Miranda had lied to her, attempting to stir up trouble.

Then a vision of the dark-haired beauty and her son came to mind. There had to be some truth to Miranda's words. Nothing else explained the existence of the child who looked so much like Braxton.

Disheartened, Dacey glanced at the clock near the door and decided it was time to return to the depot. She rose to her feet and watched as Ellie stood.

"I wanted to thank you, Ellie, for your friendship and for being the first person to make me feel welcome in town."

The woman gave her a warm hug. "You are an easy girl to like, Dacey Butler. Now, before you make me all teary-eyed, you best get on with your errands. I heard Beatrice mention something about taking you on a carriage ride this afternoon."

"Yes, I suppose I better hurry on my way. I don't want to miss out on any exciting plans." Dacey tugged gloves onto her fingers and hugged Ellie again before she rushed out the door and wandered back through town to the depot.

When she entered the ticket office, Mr. Jones glanced up at her as he helped several customers at the counter.

Once the line cleared, she stepped up to the counter and he handed over her valise. "Are you sure you must make this trip today, Miss Butler?"

"Absolutely certain, Mr. Jones, but I thank you for your concern."

He nodded his head and turned to the next customer.

Dacey took a seat on a hard wooden bench near the stove and soaked up the warmth. Absently, she wondered if she'd ever feel as warm and secure as she had at Bramble Hall. Even growing up on the ranch, she'd never experienced such a sense of belonging.

Desperate for a distraction, she picked up a discarded newspaper from the previous day and read the front page.

She noticed an advertisement for the Crystal Palace with a drawing of a beautiful lamp that guaranteed remarkable goods including crockery, lamps, household furnishings, and glassware.

An advertisement for the Bon Marche promised new novelties arrived daily that were both beautiful and cheap.

Dacey grinned at the choice of wording in the listing and continued perusing the page. An announcement for a furniture store inviting customers to come by to see their new stock caused her to reread it when she noticed a line promoting undertaking as a special feature. Disturbed by the morbid thoughts that generated, she looked outside as the train rolled into the station.

She stood and watched passengers disembark before the call came to board. She nodded once more to Mr. Jones then hurried to find a seat near a window. Although it wasn't a long trip, she wanted to watch the landscape on her way to Hendersonville.

The train chugged away from the station on time, much to her relief. Every moment she spent in town, she worried that someone from Bramble Hall might appear and demand an explanation for her abrupt departure.

Dacey settled into her seat, mentally closing another chapter of her life. She would have to write Josephine, Della, India, and Chevonne as soon as she acquired a new position and update her former roommates on what had transpired.

The train had traveled only a few miles when she glanced out the window and watched a rider approach on a fast moving horse. The man waved, trying to catch the engineer's attention, then finally gave up. He rode the horse beside one of the cars ahead of Dacey. She saw him reach out to grasp the railing above a set of steps.

Afraid they were about to be the victims of a robbery, she joined others in the car as they tried to see if the man managed to board the train.

It didn't take long until a hatless man opened the door to their car and studied the faces of the occupants.

Dacey sucked in a gulp of air when Braxton's silvery gaze collided with hers. Purposeful, he marched down the aisle as she looked around for a means of escape. With none available, she wanted to squirm or hide beneath the seat when he stopped next to her.

His eyes held a mixture of hurt, anger, disappointment, and confusion as he sank down beside her.

"What are you doing?" she hissed, aware that every set of eyes in the train car stared at them.

"Apparently, I'm going with you to Hendersonville to talk to a horse buyer." Braxton unhurriedly removed one leather glove then the other, stuffing them into his coat pocket. "At least that was the story Mr. Jones told me when I arrived at the depot."

The reaction of her traitorous body to Braxton unsettled her. While her mouth watered at the familiar welcome scent of him, the heat of his presence penetrated her side, leaving her warm and languid. Her heart cheered that he'd sought her out.

Panic set in when she realized he must have come expecting payment for all his family had done for her since she arrived at Bramble Hall. With only a few dollars left to her name, there was no possibility she could pay him back, especially given the exorbitant amount of money his mother had spent on clothes and accessories for her.

The conductor rushed into the car and hurried over to Braxton. After he paid the fare for a ticket, the man left, grumbling about young lovers being the death of him.

Braxton fixed his gaze on her again. "I ought to turn you over my lap and paddle your sweet little backside for leaving as you did."

Men seated around them snickered at Braxton's words.

Mortified, Dacey stared out the window and held her tongue, doing her best to ignore the handsome man sitting next to her.

Finally, he reached over and took her hand in his. She tried to jerk away, but he held fast. "Why did you leave Bramble Hall, Dacey?"

The sound of his deep voice, especially when he said her name, made her temperature climb.

When she remained silent, his thumb rubbed tantalizing circles across her palm. Wholly entranced with the sensation, she forgot to pull away, to fight him.

"Why did you leave me?" At his wounded tone, she looked at Braxton and fell into the stormy depths of his eyes.

"I had to." She forced herself to look away but the magnetic draw of his presence was too much and she faced him again, soaking up every feature of his beloved face.

"Did someone say something last night that upset you? Tell me the truth." Braxton studied her for a moment. His face softened while his voice lowered. "I thought we both enjoyed the ball, especially what happened outside."

"I did. I was, until..." She snapped her mouth shut.

"Until what? I'm not leaving you alone until you tell me what happened. If it takes the whole train ride to Hendersonville, then so be it. If I have to follow you around for days on end, I'll do it." Braxton bumped his leg against hers and grinned. "You know I don't give up easily."

"No, you don't," Dacey agreed. A sigh that carried her pain and loss worked free from her chest and hung between them for a long moment while she gathered her thoughts. "If you must know, someone shared a number of rather revealing facts about your nature and mentioned your tendency toward indecent habits. Quite simply, I concluded the best course of action was to immediately leave Asheville."

Braxton frowned. "Did the person sharing these so called facts happen to be Miranda Beaudry?"

Dacey gaped at him, wondering how he knew she'd spoken to the woman. "Yes."

"That doesn't surprise me. She's been full of spite and vengeance since I refused to marry her last spring."

"But she said you…" Dacey couldn't bring herself to say the words.

"I what? That I ruined her? That I sullied her sparkling reputation? That I did unspeakable things?" Braxton experienced a degree of gratification when Dacey appeared appalled by his questions. "The truth of the matter is that Father insisted I take her to a soiree and after the one evening we spent attending the festivities, she wouldn't take no for an answer. I paid court to her for a short time then I couldn't take it anymore. When I bid her goodbye, she concocted a story she thought would force me into marriage, but she'd woven the same web of lies before and no one believed her."

"I see." Dacey stared at her lap, wondering if she dared believe Braxton. He looked and sounded so sincere.

"I don't believe you do, Dacey. I'd never do any of the things she claimed. Not ever." Braxton tilted his head beneath the wide brim of her western hat and stirred the air near her ear with his breath. "There's only and ever been one woman who captured my interest and my heart."

"I know. I saw her last night and again this morning."

Perplexed, Braxton sat upright. "What? Who are you talking about?"

"There was a beautiful woman with dark hair at the ball. She had a young son. I saw you and your mother with her. It's obvious he's yours, Braxton. How can you say Miss Beaudry lied when you so clearly have a mistress and a son?"

Shocked speechless, the air whooshed out of Braxton and he released Dacey's hand. After forking his fingers through his hair and leaning forward with his elbows on his knees for several minutes, he sat back and took her hand in his again.

"If you were a man, I'd pop you in the nose for making such an assumption and besmirching my character." Braxton tempered his words with a teasing grin. "I can see how you arrived at such an outlandish conclusion though, especially with Miranda's tasteless implications. Honestly, I thought Mother told you. I suppose I should have mentioned it myself."

Frustrated and confused, Dacey glared at him. "Told me what? That she wants you to wed even though you have no need for a wife? I'm perfectly clear on that fact."

Much to her dismay, Braxton chuckled. "So was I until you wandered into my life and took up residence in my heart, Dacey Jo Butler."

It was her turn to sit speechless and stare at him.

He shrugged his broad shoulders as sadness filled his eyes. "I had a brother, William. He died four years ago in a tragic accident. He was hunting with friends and a gun accidentally discharged, killing him almost instantly. It upset Mother and Father so badly, they dealt with his death by removing every reminder of his existence. There isn't a single photograph of him at Bramble Hall and no one dares mention his name."

"Oh, Brax, I didn't know. I'm so sorry." Dacey squeezed the hand that still held hers. "What about that woman and her child? He looks just like you."

"That's because he's my nephew. Charlotte was married to William. He died eight months before Billy was born. Charlotte stayed with us until the baby arrived. When he was three months old, she returned to her family in Greenville. Eventually, she fell in love with a good man, and remarried." He gave her a long look. "I meant to introduce you last night, but Charlotte arrived late and then I couldn't find you. Although her husband couldn't get away, she and Billy will stay at Bramble Hall for a few weeks."

Unable to speak around her tears, Dacey didn't know what to say, how to apologize to Braxton for jumping to conclusions without giving him an opportunity to explain.

"Mother is beside herself that you left." Braxton resumed rubbing tantalizing circles across her palm. "Cornelia and Caroline both burst into tears and Father stormed around the house barking orders to send out every able body to search for you. My feelings were quite hurt that you didn't leave a note for me. You wrote such a lovely one for Mother and another for Cornelia."

Dacey chewed her bottom lip. How could she tell Braxton she loved him and that was the reason she couldn't write a letter. She knew the feelings in her heart would work their way through the ink of the pen, boldly announcing the truth on the written page.

"I thought you cared for me, Dacey Jo."

Tears stung the backs of her eyes as she turned to him. "I do, Braxton. Very much."

"Then how could you leave without saying goodbye? Without finding out the truth? Why did you run away?"

"Because I love you."

Sparks ignited in his gray eyes as they went from stormy to liquid silver. A slow, easy grin spread across his face. "That's good news, because I'm in love with you."

Dacey ignored the tears trailing down her cheeks as Braxton held her gaze. He released her hand and bracketed her face between his palms. "I love you with all my heart. If you'll stop this running away nonsense, we could plan a wedding. After all, that is the reason you came to Asheville. It's about time I upheld my end of the bargain."

She blinked, unable to speak around the delirious joy clogging her throat. Every dream she'd had about love and a happy ever after was about to come true.

Braxton's thumbs brushed away her tears. "Will you please come back to Bramble Hall with me? Will you come home, honey, and be my wife?"

Dacey nodded and closed her eyes as Braxton removed her hat then lowered his head to hers, gently caressing her lips.

Heedless to the train car full of people watching, he rested his forehead against hers. "Mother thinks a wedding the Saturday before Thanksgiving would be perfect. What do you think? Will you marry me in a week?"

"Yes, Braxton! Of course I'll marry you! I'd marry you right this minute if it could be arranged."

A chuckle rumbled out of his chest and he kissed her nose. "Don't tease me like that. Mother would have my head if we returned already wed." He wrapped his arm around her and pulled her against his side, settling back into the seat. "It will sorely test my patience to keep my hands and lips off you for another week, but you, my lovely mail-order bride, are worth the wait."

Chapter Twelve

"Your handsome husband-to-be asked me to bring you this," Charlotte said, handing Dacey an envelope.

She smiled at her new friend and lifted the flap. As she read it, she laughed.

"What is it? What did Braxton write?" Charlotte asked.

Dacey looked up and grinned at Charlotte then Beatrice. "He composed his own mail-order bride advertisement."

"He didn't!" Beatrice appeared amused as she helped Cornelia fasten the last of the buttons down the back of Dacey's white silk wedding gown. "Well, darling, you must read it to us."

"No. I couldn't." Dacey's cheeks pinked, but she held out the paper so the women could read it over her shoulder.

Dearest Dacey,

Since Mother wrote the first one, I thought I better pen my own advertisement for a bride. I don't exactly know what words she used to convince you to come to Asheville, but I hope these will mean you'll stay forever by my side.

Wanted: One beautiful, spunky, brave girl with hair the color of autumn's most glorious crown and eyes the shade of bottomless lakes. Must possess a sense of humor, have a way with horses that surpasses the ability of this man, and be incredibly sweet and kind-hearted. She must also be willing to put up with a strong-willed, opinionated husband who will love her so thoroughly and completely, she will wonder how she possibly survived so long without the warmth of his touch and the flavor of his kiss.

Since you clearly meet all the criteria, if you are interested in becoming my bride, please proceed to the rotunda room when the harp music begins and profess your undying devotion to the man who loves you with every beat of his heart, now and forevermore.

Your humble servant,

Braxton

Charlotte giggled and nudged her with an elbow to her side as she helped pin roses into her hair. "Brother Braxton is quite a romantic."

"Yes, he is," Dacey said, furiously blushing.

"What a wonderful note." Beatrice beamed at her as she picked up a veil and settled it on Dacey's head amidst the roses. "You must keep it for your daughters to read on their wedding day."

Dacey's eyes filled with tears and she struggled to keep her composure.

"It's okay, sweetheart." Beatrice gave her a warm hug. "He really does love you to the point of distraction."

"I know," Dacey whispered as Charlotte brushed away her tears so she wouldn't stain the fingers of her satin gloves.

"No more tears. Today is one meant to be filled with joy." Beatrice kissed her cheek and winked at her, affecting a western twang. "I reckon I better git downstairs and start pluckin' the harp." Beatrice offered one more encouraging hug before she rushed out the door.

Cornelia and Caroline adjusted Dacey's train and veil, accompanying her and Charlotte to the staircase near the rotunda room.

When the soft strains of the harp drifted up to them, Charlotte gave her an encouraging smile then gracefully walked down the steps as Dacey's attendant.

As Dacey began her descent to where Daniel waited to walk her into the room, she sent up a prayer of gratitude that she'd answered the advertisement for a wife for an Asheville farmer. She hoped her friends had found as much happiness in their new beginnings as she had in hers.

Daniel smiled as she placed her hand on his arm. "You look beautiful, dear girl. Welcome to our family."

"Thank you, sir."

Once they stepped into the room, bedecked with flowers, organza, and hundreds of candles, Dacey had eyes only for her handsome groom. Braxton took her breath away as she floated down the aisle to him.

A delighted shiver of anticipation stole over her as she stopped beside him.

He bent his head by her ear as Daniel handed her over to his keeping. "My beloved," he whispered in a voice thick with emotion.

When she smiled at him with love shining from her face, Braxton's heart overflowed with love.

Although at the time, he'd been quite irritated with his mother for meddling in his life by sending for a mail-order bride, he was glad she had. If it weren't for her scheming, he never would have met Dacey.

A life without her in it was inconceivable.

As the pastor pronounced them man and wife, the setting sun filled the room with a brilliant display, wrapping the occupants in a golden cocoon of light.

Braxton lifted Dacey's veil. His gaze traveled over her face, taking in the glow in her eyes, the pink of her cheeks, the beckoning ripeness of her lips.

Tenderly, his mouth caressed hers in a sweet, gentle kiss. Before he raised his head, he leaned toward her ear.

"That was to please those here, but I promise the kisses I'll lavish upon you later are for our pleasure alone."

"I'll hold you to that promise, buster." Dacey winked at him as they turned to face those gathered around them.

After an elaborate dinner and an hour of dancing, Braxton took Dacey by the hand and led her out of the room.

"What are you doing, Brax?" She asked as he swept her into his arms and started up the stairs.

"Isn't it obvious? I'm stealing you away." He kissed her cheek as he rushed up the steps and turned down a hall.

"Then by all means, continue," she said, trailing teasing kisses across his neck.

He groaned and tightened his hold as he strode to the end of hall then toed open a door with his foot.

"What's this room?" Dacey asked as he stepped inside and set her down. The wing they were in was secluded from the main part of the house. The large bedroom was part of the rotunda with curved windows catching the last rays of the sunset.

A massive bed and ornately carved furnishings filled the space, done in shades of ivory and green, similar to her room in the main wing of the house.

"This will be our room, honey, if you like it. Mother agreed we need a little privacy and I thought you'd enjoy the light in this room. There's a balcony where we can sit and watch the sunsets."

Braxton led her over to a door that opened to a finely appointed bathroom then he showed her the closet where Cornelia had already moved all her things.

Dacey wrapped her arms around his neck and gave him a hug. "It's perfect, Braxton. Perfect and so appreciated. Thank you."

His lips connected with hers in a fiery, heated exchange. When he finally lifted his head, Dacey clung to the lapels of his coat to keep herself upright.

After a kiss to her nose, he chuckled and stepped behind her, starting the process of unbuttoning her dress. He could have sent for Cornelia to do it, but he'd thought of doing little else since Dacey floated down the aisle on his father's arm in the enchanting gown.

"I have one more surprise for you," Braxton said as he struggled to work the buttons free. He considered tugging on the fabric and popping off the buttons, but he knew Dacey wouldn't appreciate it if he ruined her dress. There was also a bit of enticing delight in unfastening each one.

"You've done so much already. I can't imagine anything else you could give me." She turned and smiled at him over her shoulder, making his heart leap into a frenzied pounding in his chest.

He stopped fiddling with the buttons long enough to take an envelope from his coat pocket and hand it to her.

"What's this?" she asked, opening the flap.

"Just read it."

When she finished, she turned around and stared at Braxton. "You bought the ranch? My ranch?"

At his nod, she threw herself into his arms, laughing and crying as she hugged him tightly. "Oh, Brax! This is the best, best gift you could ever give me."

As thoughts assailed her, she pulled back. "I know we'll live here, but how will… what can…"

"I have it all worked out, Dacey Jo. Don't fret. Your friend Rowdy has agreed to take over management of the ranch again and he has assured me most of the hands you knew will work there again. I've transferred funds into an account for him to take care of the place and he will provide a monthly report." Braxton smiled as he brushed away a lingering teardrop from her cheek with his thumb. "I assured him we'd need to make a trip in the spring to check on our holdings. You'll also be relieved to know that your stepfather was sent to prison after he killed someone who accused him of cheating at cards."

Unable to speak through the emotion clogging her throat, Dacey nodded her head and hugged her husband again.

"I think we'll need to make a yearly trip to visit the ranch, check on things. Who knows? Maybe one of our sons will want to live there someday."

"Maybe one will." Dacey gazed up at her husband with a coy look that scattered his sense. "With your mother talking about us having daughters and you convinced we'll have sons, we best get started on creating our family."

He grinned and gently kissed her eyes, her forehead, her cheeks. "I'm more than willing to do my part."

Utter devotion filled her face as she looked up at him. "You're the finest man I've ever met, Braxton Douglas. I love you and I'm honored you chose me to love."

"The honor is all mine, honey." Fire glowed in his silvery eyes as his hands lingered at her sides.

When she pressed against him, he lost the tentative hold he'd maintained on his patience.

Braxton tugged away the remaining buttons and freed Dacey from her gown, lifting her in his arms. "Just promise you'll never change. I don't want or need a bride who sits around the house learning needlepoint or perfecting her manners. I need you — a true partner."

Happier than she'd ever been in her life, Dacey wrapped her hands around Braxton's neck and drew his mouth to hers.

In that moment, as their souls connected, she knew the rapture of loving a man such as Braxton, of being loved by him.

No longer alone in the world, Dacey's home was in his arms.

The End

Apple Pumpkin Butter

Dacey loved Apple Butter from the first moment she tasted it. Here's a simple, easy recipe for Apple Butter with an autumn twist.

Apple Pumpkin Butter
1 can (15 oz) of pumpkin
1 cup apple (peeled, cored and grated)
1 cup apple juice
½ cup brown sugar, packed
1 tablespoon of pumpkin pie spice

Combine all ingredients in a heavy-bottomed saucepan; bring to a boil on medium-high heat. Reduce heat to low and simmer for 1½ hours, stirring occasionally.

Serve on bread, biscuits, pound cake, or use as a dessert topping.

Makes three cups. Keep refrigerated.

Author's Note

It is an honor to be part of the American Mail-Order Brides project. There are 45 participating authors, covering all 50 states (some wrote two books).

When I was asked to join in the fun, the states where I typically base my stories were already taken, so I looked at the list of available options.

North Carolina jumped out at me. You see, my paternal grandfather's family came from North Carolina and I've always wondered what it would be like to live there.

Because I'm also fascinated with the Biltmore Estate (and it is on my bucket list to see someday), I thought it would be fun to set the story in Asheville, where the Biltmore resides.

As I researched the setting for this story, I happened upon a few things that were immensely helpful.

One was a photo of the Nottoway Plantation in Louisiana. I loosely based Bramble Hall on this beautiful plantation. And yes, I added it to my list of places to visit.

The other extremely helpful thing I discovered was through the Library of Congress, I could download the Asheville Daily Citizen newspaper from 1890. This helped me glimpse into daily life in the town and provided the grounds for the mention of Dacey looking at the paper. There really was an ad for a furniture store offering undertaking services. I wonder if coffins were displayed next to the settees or end tables.

I also found myself frequently visiting Explore Asheville's website.

And a thank you to Kandi B. for the fun suggestion of a weeping beech tree as a place for a romantic first kiss. Although Braxton and Dacey didn't kiss beneath the branches of the tree, they sure came close to sharing their first kiss there.

For those of you who are <u>Pendleton Petticoats</u> fans, don't you think it would be fun for one of Dacey and Braxton's children to take over the ranch? Hmm…

If you aren't familiar with the Pendleton Petticoats series, the first book in the series is Aundy.

Pendleton Petticoats Series

Set in the western town of Pendleton, Oregon, right at the turn of the 20th century, each book in this series bears the name of the heroine, all brave yet very different.

Aundy (Book 1) Aundy Thorsen, a stubborn mail-order bride, finds the courage to carry on when she's widowed before ever truly becoming a wife, but opening her heart to love again may be more than she can bear.

Caterina (Book 2) — Running from a man intent on marrying her, Caterina Campanelli starts a new life in Pendleton, completely unprepared for the passionate feelings stirred in her by the town's incredibly handsome deputy sheriff.

Ilsa (Book 3) — Desperate to escape her wicked aunt and an unthinkable future, Ilsa Thorsen finds herself on her sister's ranch in Pendleton. Not only are the dust and smells more than she can bear, but Tony Campanelli seems bent on making her his special project.

Marnie *(Book 4)* — Beyond all hope for a happy future, Marnie Jones struggles to deal with her roiling emotions when U.S. Marshal Lars Thorsen rides into town, tearing down the walls she's erected around her heart.

Lacy (Book 5) — Bound by tradition and responsibilities, Lacy has to choose between the ties that bind her to the past and the unexpected love that will carry her into the future.

Bertie *(Book 6) — The next adventure in the Pendleton Petticoat Series — coming in 2016!*

Crumpets and Cowpies **(Baker City Brides, Book 1)** — Rancher Thane Jordan reluctantly travels to England to settle his brother's estate only to find he's inherited much more than he could possibly have imagined.

Lady Jemma Bryan has no desire to spend a single minute in Thane Jordan's insufferable presence much less live under the same roof with the handsome, arrogant American. Forced to choose between poverty or marriage to the man, she finds herself traveling across an ocean and America to reach his ranch in Oregon.

Thimbles and Thistles *(Baker City Brides, Book 2)* — Maggie Dalton has no need for a man in her life. Widowed more than ten years, she's built a successful business and managed quite well on her own in the bustling town of Baker City, Oregon.

Aggravated by her inability to block thoughts of the handsome lumber mill owner from her mind, she renews her determination to resist his attempts at friendship.

The Christmas Bargain *(Hardman Holidays, Book 1)* - As owner and manager of the Hardman bank, Luke Granger is a man of responsibility and integrity in the small 1890s Eastern Oregon town. When he calls in a long overdue loan, Luke finds himself reluctantly accepting a bargain in lieu of payment from the shiftless farmer who barters his daughter to settle his debt.

The Christmas Token *(Hardman Holidays, Book 2)* - Determined to escape an unwelcome suitor, Ginny Granger flees to her brother's home in Eastern Oregon for the holiday season. Returning to the community where she spent her childhood years, she plans to relax and enjoy a peaceful visit. Not expecting to encounter the boy she once loved, her exile proves to be anything but restful.

The Christmas Calamity *(Hardman Holidays Book 3)* - Dependable and solid, Arlan Guthry relishes his orderly life as a banker's assistant in Hardman, Oregon. His uncluttered world tilts off kilter when the beautiful and enigmatic prestidigitator Alexandra Janowski arrives in town, spinning magic and trouble in her wake as the holiday season approaches.

The Christmas Vow *(Hardman Holidays Book 4)* - Adam Guthry returns home to bury his best friend and his past, never expecting to fall in love with Tia Devereux, the woman who destroyed his heart.

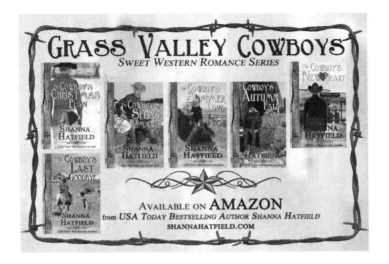

Grass Valley Cowboys Series

Meet the Thompson family of the Triple T Ranch in Grass Valley, Oregon.
Three handsome brothers, their rowdy friends, and the women who fall for them are at the heart of this contemporary western romance series.

Book 1 – *The Cowboy's Christmas Plan*
Book 2 – *The Cowboy's Spring Romance*
Book 3 – *The Cowboy's Summer Love*
Book 4 – *The Cowboy's Autumn Fall*
Book 5 – *The Cowboy's New Heart*
Book 6 - *The Cowboy's Last Goodbye*

The Women of Tenacity Series

Welcome to Tenacity!

Tenacious, sassy women tangle with the wild, rugged men who love them in this contemporary western romance series.

The paperback version offers a short story introduction, *A Prelude*, followed by the three full-length novels set in the fictional town of Tenacity, Oregon.

Book 1 – ***Heart of Clay***
Book 2 – ***Country Boy vs. City Girl***
Book 3 – ***Not His Type***

ABOUT THE AUTHOR

SHANNA HATFIELD spent ten years as a newspaper journalist before moving into the field of marketing and public relations. Self-publishing the romantic stories she dreams up in her head is a perfect outlet for her lifelong love of writing, reading, and creativity. She and her husband, lovingly referred to as Captain Cavedweller, reside in the Pacific Northwest.

Shanna loves to hear from readers.
Connect with her online:
Blog: shannahatfield.com
Facebook: Shanna Hatfield's Page
Pinterest: Shanna Hatfield
Email: shanna@shannahatfield.com

If you'd like to know more about the characters in any of her books,
visit the Book Characters page on her website or check out her **Book Boards** on Pinterest.

Made in the USA
San Bernardino, CA
01 February 2016